Shores of Chaos: Shipwrecked

Shores of Chaos: Shipwrecked

Genavieve Blackwood

BCID 377-16820832
www.bookcrossing.com

This book is a work of fiction. While historical events, real people, and real places are referred to, they are used in a fictitious manner. All other characters, places, events, and dialogue are the products of the author's imagination, and any resemblance to actual events or people, living or dead, is entirely coincidental.

Copyright © 2022 by Genavieve Blackwood

All rights reserved. No part of this book may be reproduced in any form without written permission of the author.

Independently published.

The text of this book is set in Garamond.

ISBN: 9798843405915

First Edition

*Dedicated to my father, William,
My traveling buddy and constant supporter*

CHAPTER 1- HIDDEN IN THE ROCKS

The ocean can be a thing of magnificent beauty or a powerful tormentor for all seafarers who dare traverse her. Many a soul has been lost to the treacherous depths, and if those souls could talk, and sometimes they do, they would undoubtedly share their tales of woe. To prevent more tragedies, majestic lighthouses came into being the world over to protect mariners on the open seas. In more ways than one, these beacons of light are often the only things standing between safety and the certain death that awaits all who travel on the mighty waves.

One of these lighthouses stands at Wawenock Point on the coast of Maine, not far from where the Penobscot River empties into the sea. The whitewashed brick lighthouse stands fifty-nine feet tall atop rocky cliffs at the edge of a dense pine forest. The location it watches over was named for the Wawenock Indians who once roamed these shores.

On this day, two young girls were doing the same. Anna and Marie Ashman made their way from the keeper's quarters to the edge of the cliffs.

"Hurry!"

Anna's call filled the summer air as the six-year-old ran across the grass to the cliffs. Her older sister, ten-year-old Marie, raced behind her. Their golden curls flared out behind them as they ran. The morning was warm on this early summer day of 1898. The girls were ready to embrace the carefree season before the new school year began. Their father, Edward, the resident head lighthouse keeper, watched his daughters from atop the cliffs, a weary smile on his face. Normally he would be asleep for most of the day, preparing for his nightly duties of manning the light, but he decided to spare some time to spend with his daughters. Besides, the assistant keeper, Harry Bancroft, had the first shift this evening, which would allow Edward some more time to sleep.

When the family first came here four years ago, Edward was the assistant to his uncle, who, thanks to some good old-fashioned nepotism, helped him get the job. When his uncle told him about the job opening, he jumped at the opportunity, as he had always loved the sea and thought it would bring some meaning to his career if he was able to help people. It was right around the time his father died, and working with his uncle made him feel like he was with his father again, as the two brothers had been close and very much alike. Two years ago, his uncle had a debilitating stroke that left him incapable of performing his duties, giving Edward the position of head keeper by default. Normally, such a promotion could take several years.

"Be careful on the rocks!" Edward yelled. His hazel eyes had been following his daughters the whole time and he knew where they were headed. They had gone down to the little beach dozens of times before, but he still always got nervous.

The girls reached the edge of the cliffs and scaled their way down to the small stretch of beach. It was an odd feature of the place where they lived in that the entire coastline was made of rock with the exception of this little valley of sand where the cliffs opened up. The two girls went straight to the water, where gentle waves were lapping at the sand, leaving foam in their wake. Anna stuck her feet in first as the tide came up and slowly receded. The water was cold, but refreshing. Their heavy woolen bathing dresses were sweltering in the June heat, but the breeze coming off the ocean cooled their skin. Marie came to stand beside her sister and dipped her toes into the water. Marie was more than willing to sit by the waves and enjoy their comings and goings, but Anna was not so easily contented. She started walking to the left, stepping on a low slab of rock.

"Where are you going?" Marie asked.

"I'm going to look for a cave," she responded.

"I told you there are no caves around here!" Marie was becoming increasingly impatient with her sister's desire to find a cave. Ever since Margaret, Harry's wife, had told them a story about a mermaid who lived in a cave by the seashore, Anna had been convinced there was a cave near the keeper's quarters.

Anna let out a dissatisfied grunt. "You don't know that for sure!" She turned from her older sister and continued climbing up the rocks.

"You know Father doesn't like us going on the rocks," Marie reminded her.

"I will be careful," Anna returned without looking

back.

Marie looked back at their father warily. He was a kind man, but could be very stern. You did not want to invoke his wrath. "I don't think that's a good idea!"

"I'm going and you can't stop me!" The little one was insistent. Once Anna set her mind to something, it was nearly impossible to change it. She and Marie couldn't be more different. While Marie was quiet, intellectual, and would be content with reading a good book, Anna was rambunctious, headstrong, and always looking for an adventure. Anna bent down and began to climb on all fours for a better grip as she moved along a steeper rock. Marie didn't want to, but she decided to follow Anna, if for no other reason than to make sure her sister did not hurt herself.

Just as Marie stepped on one of the rocks, she heard her father's voice. "Do not climb on the rocks!"

"I told you he'd get mad!" Marie yelled at her sister. "Come back now!"

"Goody Two-shoes!" Anna mocked her sister as she continued to move along the rocks.

"Anna, you're going to get it!"

"Anna!"

Their father's stern voice from atop the cliff finally made Anna pause. She sighed and turned to go back to the beach. "Fine! I'll just sit on the sand and be bored," she muttered.

Marie shook her head and bent over to pick up seashells. She dug into the sand when she saw a mussel shell sticking up. When she freed the mussel, she held it up to show Anna. "Look! This one has both halves!"

Anna, who was sitting on the beach with her arms folded, just huffed and turned the other way. Marie ignored her and continued looking for shells. She found a large clam shell and few other broken bits of various shells here and there. She really wanted to find a sand dollar, but never had any luck.

Meanwhile, Anna was looking to her right, staring at the other side of the rocks. She squinted as the sunlight glinted off the waves. Then something caught her gaze. There was something wavering by the rocks as the waves came in and out. It looked like a dead fish flopping around in the water. She got up to take a closer look and had to climb over some large rocks to do so.

Marie looked up and couldn't believe her sister was climbing the rocks again. "Anna, get back on the beach!" she scolded. When the younger girl didn't move, Marie yelled again. "Don't ignore me!" Anna didn't respond and instead just stood staring down between the rocks. Marie stalked over the rocks and grabbed her sister's arm, attempting to pull her back, but Anna seemed frozen to the spot. Marie found this odd as Anna would usually snap at her with some snarky reply. "Anna?" Marie asked in concern. Then she followed her sister's gaze to the spot in between the rocks that she had been looking at.

Edward let out an exasperated sigh as he saw his daughters walking on the rocks again and started to walk toward the cliffs. If they couldn't listen then they couldn't play on the beach. This was the family's fourth year at the light and while the girls had become familiar with the shoreline and the rhythm of the ocean tides, he still feared for their safety. They knew it was dangerous to climb on the rocks so it angered him that they weren't listening.

"Why are they over there? You know I don't want

them on the rocks." The sound of his wife's voice stopped him in his tracks.

"I'm going to get them now," he answered her, but did not bother to turn around. He did not want to look at her. Every time he faced Frances he was filled with intense dread. He could no longer stand the sight of the dark circles under her eyes and her unkempt hair. She stopped seeming to care at all about her appearance. Sometimes she appeared to be two different people. Half the time she barely left their bedroom, spending most of her day sitting at the window, staring out at the shoreline with needlework in her hands, but seemingly nothing in her mind. At other times she would be fretting about, worrying about making sure things were done exactly right, and she would become irritable if someone did something wrong or tried to interfere.

"He won't stop crying." The mention of their two-month-old son, Thomas, filled him with even more dread. It was childbirth that had caused this never-ending melancholy she was in. Two years earlier, before Thomas was born, she had miscarried. The loss had greatly upset her, and when she finally seemed to be better, Edward had foolishly thought that having another baby would soothe her, but it only made her worse. After he was born, it seemed like she had to force herself to hold him or feed him. It broke Edward's heart to see his son crying for his mother's affection and never receiving it.

He finally turned to look at her and instantly regretted it. Her eyes were puffy and red. She'd been crying … again. A shawl was draped limply around her shoulders. Her already thin frame seemed to become smaller every day. She no longer ate with the same voracity as she had. And he knew she didn't sleep well either, sometimes seeing the light from the windows of their bedroom from up in the lighthouse at night. To him, she seemed more like a frail old lady than the vibrant, beautiful woman he had married.

"Let Margaret take care of him then," he told her, although he was sure that the other woman was just as exhausted as he was. His wife's current state, and his own limitations to help due to his work schedule, forced Margaret to take care of the children most of the time. Even though Margaret never complained, he would often see the disdainful looks she would sometimes give Frances, angry that she was of no help in doing anything around the household. Edward did his best to help when he could and started doing small things around the quarters that Frances would normally do, but he found himself growing tired of it and began to start his shifts early each night to escape into his job.

"I had to leave the house," she stated bluntly. "I couldn't stand listening to him cry another moment."

He just shook his head and turned from her. He did not know what to do anymore. Part of him tried to be sympathetic to her sadness and another part of him just wanted to shake her and scream at her to pull herself together. Every attempt he made to talk to her about it ended with her crying or yelling at him that he didn't understand. Of course he didn't; not when she hardly communicated her feelings. He would end up just leaving her alone, but he was beginning to believe that would no longer be an option. He could no longer ignore the problem when it was becoming worse every day and he had no way of fixing it.

His thinking was interrupted by the screams of his

daughters. He looked in their direction and ran toward them. "I told you not to let them by the rocks!" Frances screamed as loudly as the girls.

"Father! Father!" Marie screamed as she scrambled to reach the top of the rocky cliff. "There's a man in the rocks!"

Not quite comprehending what his daughter was saying, he asked, "What? What man?" He held out his hand for Marie to take and then extended the other to Anna.

"There's a man by the rocks!" Anna answered for her sister. She pointed to a spot in the shoreline.

Frances had come over to see what the commotion was about, and both girls made their way to her and clung to her skirts. "What's going on? Edward?" She looked at her husband.

"I'm not sure." He grappled his way down to where Anna had pointed. He could see something moving in the water, but a large rock was obstructing his view. Getting closer to the rock, he stopped when he finally realized what had frightened his daughters. "My God," he gasped. Wedged between two rocks, with his legs swaying in time with the waves, was a dead man.

CHAPTER 2- DANGEROUS WATERS

Following the discovery of the dead man, Edward alerted the proper authorities. Port DePaix, the town that Wawenock Point was a part of, sent several police officers and a detective to investigate. Two policemen took statements from Edward and Harry and briefly asked Marie and Anna some questions, as they had seen the body first. Word must have gotten out that there was a dead body because a few teenagers from town came to see it for themselves, only for the police to chase them away. Just as the police officers were finishing their investigation and the coroner was removing the body, David Wilkins, a collector of customs from the Portland customs office, showed up, much to Edward's surprise. He took a quick look at the body and then went to confer with the detective. As the police officers were leaving, the detective and Wilkins walked up to Edward and Harry. The detective spoke first.

"Forgive me for not properly introducing myself before. I'm Detective Michael Hanlon," he greeted and held out his hand.

Edward shook it and introduced himself. "Edward Ashman; I'm the head keeper."

Hanlon turned to Harry, who introduced himself as well.

"So you didn't notice any suspicious activity last night?" Hanlon asked.

"No, I didn't," Edward replied. "Just the occasional ship passing by."

"And you, Mr. Bancroft?" Hanlon looked at the older man.

"Can't say that I did."

"It's likely the man washed up then, considering the position he was found in," Hanlon explained.

"Gentlemen, I'd like to speak with you all inside if I may," Wilkins announced.

"Of course." Edward gestured for him to continue into the keeper's quarters. The four walked into the office and Edward took his seat at the desk. Harry stood in the corner while the detective and collector took the seats opposite Edward.

"The police sent a telegram to my office as soon as they found out about the body. I came as soon as I could. I'm here because we have reason to believe this man is connected to another crime," Wilkins explained. "I don't know how well you follow the news out here, but three days ago the RC *Gresham* found a ship, the *Josephine*, abandoned on a reef. It had been reported missing after it was several days late from when it was scheduled to come into port."

"No, I hadn't heard about it," Edward said.

"Neither had I," Harry agreed.

"When they found the ship, several valuable cargo items had been stolen," Wilkins continued. "But that wasn't all. Most of the crew members were found dead aboard the ship. Their throats were cut, same as the man you just found." Wilkins paused as Edward and Harry exchanged glances.

"That wasn't in the papers," Hanlon commented.

"We kept that information secret because we didn't want to cause an upset. Lord knows the press does that enough with the war in Cuba." Wilkins gave a dissatisfied grunt.

"So someone at the police station must have known the man was connected to the other crime if they informed you?" Hanlon's question came off as more of an accusation.

"Chief Bouchard is a friend," Wilkins explained. "I told him about the *Josephine* when I last spoke with him." Hanlon nodded to that, but still looked suspicious.

"So you think this man may have been one of the crew members?" Harry interrupted.

"Yes, but it makes me wonder how many more bodies we may come across." Wilkins sighed before he continued, "You see, the *Gresham*'s boarding officer found the ship's register aboard the *Josephine*. There were fourteen crew members listed for the voyage plus the captain. We found the captain and eleven crew members dead on the ship and this man you just found appears to be the twelfth. The question now is: where are the last two?"

"Floating out in the middle of the Atlantic, I suppose," Harry grumbled in his gravelly voice.

"Maybe, or we could be dealing with something more than just murder at sea." Wilkins raised an eyebrow.

"What do you mean?" Edward asked.

"Well, the fact that there are still two unaccounted for sailors made me think," he explained as he chose his words carefully. "There were two previous incidents within the last month or so that this one appears connected to. The first incident involved a ship that ran aground on some rocks and took on water in the middle of the night. The captain said his wheelman was attempting to escape the path of a small sailing boat that was headed directly toward them. They tried to command the boat to steer clear, but when it wouldn't move, the ship made a hard turn to port. The lookout says he swore there were two or three men on that sailing boat from what he could make out in the dark.

"The second incident involved a ship carrying lumber. It caught fire in the middle of the night, causing damage to most of the cargo and part of the ship. The captain said nothing like that had ever happened before and when he went to take account of all of his crew, three new men he had signed on were missing. When they searched the ship, they were nowhere to be found and no human remains were found in the scorched part of the ship. Needless to say, we think those three were arsonists and jumped ship when they committed their crime."

"So you think these two or three men were causing all of these incidents? But was there any damage to this last ship? Or only stolen cargo?" Edward wondered.

"It would appear at first glance that this one is unrelated, but the first two ships were both insured by the East Knox Insurance Company through their Rockland office. When I found out about the dead man here, I had just received confirmation that the

Josephine too was insured with that company through that office. So it seems that we have ourselves a crime syndicate whose game is insurance fraud and now murder and piracy."

"But don't the ships have different owners?" Harry asked as he twirled strands of his white beard in contemplation. He was every bit the stereotypical old sea dog. He had shaggy gray hair and wrinkles that indicated years of hard service and a gruff voice to match.

"That's the only thing that's making me scratch my head," the collector agreed. "The owners of these ships would all need to be working with this crime syndicate, which seems odd. Until we can find out more information, in the meantime, I would like you two to keep an eye out for any suspicious activity, and alert my office immediately. And Mr. Hanlon, I know the police department here has already been told to lookout for any stolen goods that may be connected to the *Josephine* should they turn up."

"Yes, it has." Hanlon stiffened. He seemed uncomfortable with the whole conversation.

Once Wilkins and Hanlon left, Edward sat down to write up a report about the man found in the rocks. Any incidents such as shipwrecks and the like had to be reported to the district inspector. After he'd described the situation with the dead man, the report took a more mundane turn as Edward made remarks about the condition of the light and the weather. He then made note in the expenditure book of how much oil had been used the previous night. *They don't pay me enough for this job,* Edward mused to himself as he ran a hand through his brown locks. Indeed, being a keeper meant more than making sure a lighthouse shone its light at night. Lightkeepers were expected to intervene should anyone at sea be in harm's way. They were also expected to make any repairs to the light and grounds when capable, something that could often be a daunting task.

After making his notes, he sat back and rubbed his eyes. He was growing weary of being a keeper. He remembered when he started as an assistant keeper and how enthusiastic he was with the daily chores that accompanied his job. But after four years on the job, he had grown bored of the tedious, repetitive tasks. He also wondered how much longer he'd be physically able to perform his duties. He was only thirty-three, but every day his body ached a bit more and he wasn't getting any younger. Plus, he now had three children and an ailing wife to add to his mental fatigue. Sometimes he wondered how men at Harry's age and even older managed to do it for so long. *God bless 'em*, he thought.

☙

That night, before sunset, Marie and Anna sat at the kitchen table waiting for Margaret to serve dinner. The woman, who was in her late fifties, bustled about the kitchen juggling pots and pans as she prepared the evening meal. Her hair, which was brown and speckled with gray strands, was up in a loose bun and beads of sweat clung to her forehead. She found it odd that the two girls were so quiet, but assumed that the sight of the dead man had shaken them. Occasionally, the girls would look up to stare at each other, trying to see if one could tell what the other was thinking, but said nothing. They both turned as their father entered the room.

"Your mother will not be joining us," he announced. Frances had come to bed just as he was getting up. She claimed she was too upset to eat and just wanted to sleep. Unfortunately, this was not a unique occurrence for her. A dead man may have caused it this time, but anything could upset her and cause her to withdraw to the safe space of the bedroom.

"She was shaking all over again," Marie commented.

He raised his eyebrows. He didn't like hearing his daughters speak that way about their mother, but he said nothing. And what could he say? That their mother was wasting away and very likely to throw herself into the ocean? His children weren't ignorant; they knew when things were amiss and it was becoming harder to excuse away their mother's unstable temperament.

"Well, she may find it hard to stop thinking of the man that was found today," Edward said. "But I need you girls to try to put him out of your mind. I do not want you to be frightened about it. It was simply an accident; they happen all the time."

"Accident?" Marie questioned. "His throat was cut."

He sighed. "Yes, if you must know the truth, he was murdered. You are too young to know such cruelties of the world, but they do indeed happen."

"Did they catch who did it?" Anna asked.

"Not yet."

"So he's still out there? What if he comes for us next?" The younger girl's eyes widened.

"Mr. Wilkins believes this crime is connected to

another set of crimes that have occurred. Someone has been going after merchant ships. It's not the work of some maniac on the loose; you have nothing to fear."

"Enough of that talk around the table," Margaret scolded as she finished preparing dinner, then called for her husband, "Harry! Dinner is ready!" When the older man made his way into the room and sat down, his wife set the plates on the table. The meal was cod with potatoes and broccoli.

Anna looked at hers in disgust. "Cod again? All we ever eat is cod and lobster, lobster and cod."

"We just had chicken on Monday," Marie reminded her.

"You should be grateful you have food on your plate," Edward reprimanded his daughter.

"That's right," Margaret said as she sat down. "When I was your age, I was living in Ireland during the famine. There were people dying in the streets because they couldn't get enough food. So be glad you have food at all."

"Indeed," Edward stated as the five of them held hands. "Bless us, Father, and thank you for this meal we are about to partake of. We pray for the soul of the man who has so recently been lost to us. Amen."

When he had finished saying grace, everyone began eating. Despite her initial disgust, Anna ate ravenously. No one said much except for Harry, who grumbled that the potatoes were too hard, to which Margaret told him to cook them himself next time. Marie had only eaten half of her food when her stomach began to feel uneasy. The image of the dead man wouldn't leave her mind, even though her father told her not to think of it. His lifeless eyes, his twisted face, the deep gash on his neck… it made her sick. "May I be excused?" she asked, looking at her father.

"You haven't finished eating," was his curt reply.

"I feel unwell," she said quietly, looking down at her plate.

Normally he would have forced her to eat everything on her plate, but given the events from earlier in the day, he was willing to make an exception this time. "Alright, you can be excused. I suppose Margaret can feed the rest to Daisy." Daisy was the name given by the girls to the gray tabby cat that roamed around the keeper's quarters, keeping it free of mice.

"Thank you." Marie got up swiftly and left the room, going to the bedroom she shared with her sister.

The others finished their meal soon after. Anna helped Margaret to clean up the table then kissed her father's cheek. "Goodnight, Papa," she said, even though she knew he would be up with his nightly duties while she and her sister were asleep.

"Goodnight," he replied as the girl left the room. He got up to help dry the dishes that Margaret had just washed.

"It is better that you tell them of the cruelties of the world now, so they do not learn it the hard way later," Margaret spoke to him.

He hated when she tried to impart her hard-earned wisdom onto him and today he was particularly in no mood for it. "I would prefer if you did not tell me how to raise *my* children."

Margaret put her hands on her filled-out hips. "Well, as a mother of six, I think I know a thing or two about rearing children. The more you teach them now, the less they have to learn later," she retorted, her Irish brogue coming out in full force.

"Ah, Peggy, don't start," Harry's gravelly voice came as he chided his wife.

"I ain't startin' nothing."

"I had to go and marry an Irishwoman, so damned stubborn."

"If it weren't for this Irishwoman you'd be six feet under!"

"I could only wish."

"Would you two stop already?" Edward interjected. He audibly sighed at their bickering and pulled money out of his back pocket. "Margaret, do you have any plans for tomorrow?"

"Nothing but the usual," she answered.

"Then would you like to go into town tomorrow with the girls?" he asked, placing the money on the counter. "Maybe to the boardwalk? They need something to take their minds off of what happened today and I would greatly appreciate the favor."

Margaret knitted her eyebrows. *As you greatly appreciate everything else I do*, she thought bitterly. She would be glad to leave the keeper's quarters for awhile, but there were still responsibilities to take care of here. "I would like to, but…" Her voice trailed off.

"But what?"

"What about the baby?" She knew all too well that Frances could not be left alone to care for the child.

"Do not worry about him, just take the girls into town and have a nice day out, please." He turned abruptly. "Goodnight," he called as he left the room.

Margaret watched as he left. She shook her head. "I suppose I am a mother of nine now," she grumbled to herself.

Harry didn't miss a beat when he said, "God help the children."

~

Because his usual sleep schedule was interrupted due to the day's events, Edward decided to take a nap for an hour or two before his shift began. He was surprised when he entered his bedroom to find Frances sitting in the rocking chair, holding Thomas. The baby was fast asleep, content in his mother's arms for a change.

"Are the girls in bed?" she asked quietly.

"Yes," he replied. He sat on the bed and took off his shoes. "Thought I would get some sleep before my shift starts."

She nodded and continued gently rocking back and forth in the chair.

"I asked Margaret to take the girls into town tomorrow. Perhaps you should go with them. Get out of the house for awhile," he lightly suggested.

She shrugged. "I don't know. I'll see how I feel tomorrow."

"Very well," he muttered and lay down.

After awhile, he heard Frances's voice. "I don't think I can stay here anymore, Edward."

"What do you mean?" He opened his eyes and looked at her.

"I don't like it here anymore," she murmured. "It's too isolated. I miss my sister."

He shook his head in frustration. He had offered to take her to visit her sister many times over the past few weeks and she had refused each time, not wanting to leave the house. "Frances, you know you can go into town or see your sister anytime you want to. You aren't a prisoner here," he said and then thought, *though you act like you are*.

"It's not the same," she muttered. "I feel like I don't belong in society anymore when I've lived all the way out here for so long." She really meant to say that she didn't feel like she belonged in her own family anymore. She felt so distant from her husband and her children, but decided not to voice her concern.

"What do you want me to do, Frances?" he asked tiredly. All he wanted to do was sleep and now she was giving him more cause for concern. "I have to work. I can't just leave."

"You can get another job," she said matter-of-factly.

"I believe that would be easier said than done."

"You are a good worker and a smart man," she stated. "It wouldn't be hard for you to find employment."

He huffed. "Frances, please, not now. It's been an exhausting day. I just want to sleep." He turned on his side and closed his eyes so he would not have to look at her straight on, but he could still hear the light sniffling that came from her direction.

CHAPTER 3- A FORTUNE TOLD

When Margaret came into Marie and Anna's bedroom the next morning to tell them to put on some nice dresses because they were going into town, the girls squealed with excitement. They hurriedly dressed and bounded down the stairs and into the kitchen. They wore identical high-necked, smocked dresses with puffy sleeves and ruffles around the yoke of the bodice, except that Marie's was light lavender and Anna's baby pink. When they sat down at the table, both wolfed down their breakfast so that they could go into town as quickly as possible.

"I know you girls are excited, but eat human bites please," Edward teased.

Frances, who had joined them this morning, gave them a small smile. "You two have fun today."

"You aren't coming?" Marie asked.

"No, I'm afraid not," she replied. "I don't feel well."

Marie nodded and continued eating. Edward said nothing. He couldn't understand her. Just last night she complained about how she couldn't stand to be here anymore, but when given the opportunity to leave, even if only for a little while, she didn't take it. When breakfast was finished, the girls hurriedly helped Margaret to clean up. They gave their parents kisses on the cheeks and rushed out the door, with Margaret trying to keep up with them.

They made their way to town on the dirt road that divided the pine forest. Wawenock Point was about a mile away from the main part of town. Port DePaix was a quaint coastal town situated between the Kennebec and Penobscot rivers. It was named after Augustin DePaix, a Frenchman of some importance during the colonial period. In the summer, Port DePaix was a seaside wonderland, for the season was celebrated in its full glory here. The port itself was busy with ships coming and going with whatever cargo they were carrying. The parks, situated near charming gingerbread-style houses, were filled with people. Young men and boys could be found playing sports while women and young ladies dressed in their best went for a nice afternoon stroll. An ice cream vendor was usually nearby, ringing his bell so that the children could come to his cart for some of the sweet cold stuff.

The boardwalk was the main draw, however. It ran parallel to a stretch of beach and had a section that turned right and went out over the ocean. There were various stores and eateries on the boardwalk and it was always bustling with people looking to buy little trinkets or get something to eat. Families could always be found sunbathing on the beach while the children splashed around in the waves. Those seeking more of a thrill could go on the amusement rides, which were some of the newer features of the boardwalk. The town was attempting to compete with Old Orchard Beach as Maine's premier tourist destination. Old Orchard had just built a steel pier that was over 1,700 feet long. It was a spectacle and would draw large crowds, so the Port DePaix town council decided to up the ante by having amusement rides installed. A new grand hotel was being built near the middle of the boardwalk as well to attract the richer clientele.

As Marie, Anna, and Margaret made their way onto the boardwalk, the sun was high in the sky and a cool breeze came from over the sea. The boardwalk was alive with many people strolling down its wood planks. A few people stood against the railings staring out across the beach to where the waves rolled in and out. Others were visiting the shops that lined the boardwalk. Some were wading into the ocean and sunbathing. The wailing of a calliope could be heard in the distance. Marie and Anna walked side by side, trying to look all around to catch everything that was happening on the boardwalk. Their straw boater hats shaded them from the scorching sun. Margaret was behind them with a parasol above her head.

"Can we go on the new Ferris wheel they put in?" Anna asked excitedly as she spotted the giant ride in the distance.

"Yes, and I want to go on the carousel," Marie said in return.

"You can go on whatever you want," Margaret answered. "Just don't expect me to go on 'em with you."

"Why, don't you like rides?" Marie taunted her good-naturedly.

"Too unenthusiastic for merry-go-rounds and too

afraid of heights for a Ferris wheel," was her blunt reply.

The girls made their way to the carousel. It was large, with several beautifully painted horses. They came in all colors and had lavish ribbons and flowers decorating their manes. Even the painted saddles had plentiful details. There were also a few benches dressed as gilded sleighs on the platform. The top of the exterior housing of the carousel was decorated with swirled woodwork and small paintings of beach and ocean scenes. One of these paintings had mermaids sitting on rocks; another a grand ship making its way through ferocious waves. Marie looked at each one intently as the carousel made its final few rotations before the current ride ended. She was mesmerized by the beautiful artwork.

As the first group of passengers left, the girls moved their way up to the entrance of the ride. The ride operator eyed the girls curiously as he took their tokens. He was a rather large man, round through the torso with a gray mustache that curled at the ends. His eyes twinkled as he spoke. "Say, you're the lightkeeper's daughters, aren't you?"

"Yes, we are," Marie answered, her interest piqued. "You know our father?"

"Know him!" the man answered with a hearty laugh. "Hell, man still owes me money from the last card game we played together!"

The girls raised their eyebrows and gave the man a look of both confusion and suspicion. "Eh, never mind about that," the man grumbled under his breath. "Now go on, pick your horses!" He waved his hand to usher them onto the ride.

Anna hurried past her sister and climbed onto a

white horse with a pale yellow mane on the outer edge of the carousel. It was decorated with magenta and purple ribbons and flowers with a saddle to match. Marie got on to the horse next to hers; a brown horse with a black mane. It had a green and blue saddle with similarly colored ribbons. The ride began and the horses bobbed up and down. Anna tried reaching out for one of the brass rings that circled the ride. Getting one of those rings meant that your next ride was free.

"Aww!" she cried out. "My arms aren't long enough!"

Marie couldn't help but laugh at her sister. "Don't worry, I'm sure you'll be taller next year to reach them," she assured the younger girl.

Margaret watched the ride as it spun around, keeping an eye on the two girls. She couldn't help but notice the carousel operator staring at her. She looked away when she caught his gaze, pretending not to notice, but she could still feel his eyes on her. She became unnerved and moved to the opposite side of the ride. As the ride came to an end, she walked to where the girls were. They got off the horses and joined the older woman and began to walk further down the boardwalk.

There were several restaurants on the boardwalk, each emitting their own unique smell.

"Something smells good!" Anna sniffed the air, trying to guess what food was making the heavenly scent.

"Can we stop and eat when we are done, Peggy?" Marie turned and looked at Margaret.

"Yes, as long as you don't spend all the money on souvenirs," she replied, a slight smirk on her face.

"Oh, we aren't that bad!" Anna yelled back, her eyebrows crossing in anger.

"Look, there's the Ferris wheel," Marie said, pointing to the tall, steel structure. "Are you sure you don't want to go on, Peggy?"

"Oh no, it's too tall," the older woman replied. "And who knows how safe it is. I don't trust all of these newfangled inventions."

"I'll take the chance!" Anna exclaimed and Marie agreed.

The girls ran to the ride and got on when the previous set of passengers left. They grinned excitedly as they rose higher in the air. Marie was busy staring out at the ocean when Anna nudged her. "Look, you can see the lighthouse from here!"

Marie looked out in the distance to where her sister was pointing. She had to squint to see the white conical structure. "It looks so small from here," she said, before turning to look at ships passing along the shoreline. She enjoyed feeling the summer breeze on her face and listening to the cheerful laughter of the people on the beach.

The ride came to an end after a few more rotations. The girls hopped down from the carriage they were in and joined Margaret on the boardwalk. They walked past several stores including a dress shop, a cigar shop, and a candy shop, which Anna begged to go in. The girls entered and looked around at the several types of colorful candies. It was like being in a candy-coated dream. Anna decided to buy taffy while Marie bought licorice, of course not without some scolding from Margaret about the dangers of overindulging in treats.

They left the store and continued walking along

the boardwalk. They came up to the Poseidon Theater where posters were displayed for the upcoming vaudeville shows. The shows were of the cleaner sort, meant as family entertainment. Normally the theater held continuous performances, in which up to six shows could be held in one day. But during the summer, when the tourists came to town, the theater held special two-shows-a-day performances on the weekends at a slightly higher price and with supposedly better acts. It was all to give the air of grander entertainment. One poster read "Saturday Night Spectaculars! Don't miss these amazing acts: The Atlantic Acrobats, The Beethoven Quartet, The Stargazer Theater Co. with the short *The Washerwoman*, Jack Porter with his beloved ventriloquist dummy Bobby Boy, and Marco the Magnificent, world famous magician!"

"Do you think Father would let us see the show?" Marie asked, looking to Anna. "I've always wanted to see one of these."

"I hope so," Anna replied. "I want to see the magician!" She said the last word slowly as she read the poster.

"You girls act like your father's made of money," Margaret continued with her incessant scolding.

"It's only fifteen cents a person!" Anna argued with her. "It's not much!"

"To you maybe." Margaret stared at the young girl, annoyed.

"Well, it doesn't hurt to ask him." Marie tried to calm the situation.

"Fine, but don't be surprised when he gets angry." Margaret was set on proving her point.

They continued walking along the boardwalk until

the girls spotted an ice cream parlor. "Can we get ice cream?" Anna turned to Margaret.

"I thought you wanted to eat at a restaurant."

"We can get ice cream after we eat lunch."

"Either lunch or ice cream; not both," she replied. "If you have lunch and ice cream you're very likely to become sick and I'm not cleaning up your vomit."

Marie cringed at how crass the woman could be sometimes. "I say we have ice cream, it would make the heat more bearable."

The other two agreed, and they all walked into the parlor, thankful for the cooler air. They sat at one of the tables that had a marble top. The chairs had cushions and ornate metal work that made up the back and legs. Next to the tables was the long counter where one could sit on a stool and order something. The counter was made of fine, darkly polished wood and had a pristine marble countertop. Several jars of ice cream toppings were on display to entice visitors to spend a few more cents to make their ice cream bowls a bit more exotic. Behind the counter were large mirrors that reflected the customers who sat in the shop. Its edges were finished in stained glass squares, the same design that bordered the windows of the parlor. The girls looked up in the mirror, staring at all that was happening behind them, trying to keep themselves entertained. A rather pleasant man in an apron and bow tie came up to their table to take their order. Marie ordered raspberry ice cream, Anna chocolate, and Margaret an ice cream soda. The girls were quiet as they savored their frozen treats, and Margaret's dessert must have been very good for she got through the whole meal without a single grumble.

They left the parlor and began walking back to the

end of the boardwalk. A man stood at the corner yelling at people nearby. A man next to him was tap dancing. His shoes made a distinctive beat against the wooden planks of the boardwalk. He was spinning around and making different melodies with his shoes.

"Come on, gather round," the first man called out in a sing-song voice. "We're the best tap dancers in town, you won't find no better sound, no matter what goes down!" He then joined his partner in dancing.

Soon a few people had gathered around the men to see what was going on. Many were talking to each other and complimenting the men on their performance. Others threw coins into the hat at the men's feet. Anna and Marie walked up to the crowd, trying to make their way to the front so they could see what was going on. The men's performance was mesmerizing and they couldn't take their eyes off them.

"Are you girls enjoying the performance?" the deep voice of a woman asked from behind them. The girls turned to look up at a woman perhaps in her mid-thirties, with dark hair and dark eyes. She wore a large amount of jewelry and a colorful paisley shawl was wrapped around her shoulders.

"Yes," Marie answered shyly.

"I am Madame Leonora, I can tell you your fortune," the woman told her, trying to give her voice a mysterious tone.

"We shouldn't participate in fortune telling," Marie told her. Growing up in a Christian household, the girls were taught not to partake in such practices.

"Well, it's not necessarily participating if you're just listening," Madame Leonora tried to reassure them.

"I want to know our fortune!" Anna jumped in.

"Very well, little one," Leonora said with amusement before continuing in a much more serious tone, "I see a darkness invading your life. Be wary of the spirits that haunt the shores of the light."

Anna's face changed from enthusiasm to complete horror and a pallor came over her features. Marie, just as frightened, grabbed her sister's arm and pulled her in the other direction. "We…we should be leaving now," Marie stuttered as she forced her legs to move.

Both girls quickly found their way to Margaret. Upon noticing the looks on their faces, she asked, "What's the matter?"

"Nothing, can we just leave now?" Marie spoke hurriedly.

Margaret eyed them both carefully, but nodded and followed the girls as they made their way back to Wawenock Point.

As Madame Leonora watched them leave, a man joined her. "Did you tell them?" the carousel operator asked her.

"Yes," she answered without looking at him.

"You didn't scare them too much, I hope?" He looked at her.

"I had to, otherwise they would not listen." She still didn't look at him.

"And do you think they'll listen?"

"If they are smart girls they will."

જી

When they returned to the keeper's quarters, Marie walked to her father's office, where he was writing in the expenditure book. She was still shaken from Madame Leonora's words, but tried to put them out of her mind. Right now she was more afraid of what her father would say when she asked about seeing the vaudeville show.

Edward looked up once he saw his daughter enter the room. "Did you have fun today?" he asked her.

"Yes, very much." She tried to put on a cheerful face.

"What did you do?" He couldn't help but notice her forced happiness.

"Anna and I went on the carousel and Ferris wheel," she answered. "Then Peggy bought us ice cream and we saw some men tap dancing."

"Sounds like a swell time." He gave her a small smile.

"It was and then we walked past the theater and we saw a poster for the new shows they have every Saturday," she explained to him. "And, well… it's just that Anna and I always wanted to see one of those shows. Marco the Magnificent is supposed to be there. I hear his act is really good."

"So you want to go," he said, smirking at her dancing around the question. "What times are the shows?"

"I believe five o'clock and eight o'clock," she answered.

"How much?"

"The cheapest seats are fifteen cents per person," she said sheepishly, afraid he might find it too high.

"That's not bad." His reply pleasantly surprised her. However, he still needed to be able to take the night off work and get permission to leave his post. "Very well, I will think about it," he said finally, not wanting to disappoint his daughter too much.

"Thank you so much for everything today," she stated.

"You're very welcome." He smiled again before adding, "Oh, and don't forget tomorrow when you are doing your chores to make sure nothing is blocking the entrances to any of the rooms. We will be having our quarterly inspection soon," he explained to her.

"Yes, sir," she answered.

"I'm glad you had fun today."

"Me too," she replied back, a sad smile on her face as Leonora's words came to her mind again.

"Are you sure there's nothing else the matter?" He quirked an eyebrow at her as she turned to leave.

"No, I'm fine." She gave a more reassuring smile over her shoulder before leaving the room.

꽃

Night had fallen over the coast and the two girls sat in their beds, both made of identical metal framework. Their beds were close to each other's in the small room. The two adult couples in the household each had a bigger room, much to the girls' annoyance. Sharing a room had proven to be quite tedious. Each girl had her own preferences and daily routine which tended to annoy the other.

For example, right now, Marie had the kerosene lamp lit and was finishing up the last few pages of a chapter in a book she was reading. Anna, though, just wanted to go to sleep and was growing increasingly exasperated.

"Will you stop reading already!" she yelled at her

sister.

"Calm yourself, I'm almost done," Marie retorted.

Anna sighed. To be honest, she probably wouldn't get much sleep anyway with Madame Leonora's words still haunting her as well. "Do you think she was serious?" she asked Marie. "You know, the fortune teller."

Marie was worried about it too, but didn't want to frighten her sister. "Of course not," she answered. "Those fortune tellers just want to scare people. I doubt she can even see anything anyway."

"Are you sure?" Anna was unconvinced.

"Yes, just say your prayers and everything will be fine," Marie told her.

"I already did."

"Then don't worry about it." Marie finished the chapter and put the book down on the nightstand. She lowered herself to the floor and said her evening prayers. Afterwards, she pulled the covers of her bed back and extinguished the kerosene lamp. She lay down and turned on her side, looking out the window to stare at the night sky. The moon glowed in the distance and a few stars hovered beside it. A light breeze drifted in through the window and the curtains flapped. The cooler air helped to remove some of the heat from the room. Marie kicked up her cotton nightgown to her knees to further allow the air to cool her body.

She closed her eyes and tried to sleep, but found it impossible. *I see a darkness invading your life. Be wary of the spirits that haunt the shores of the light.* Madame Leonora's words echoed in her mind. The thought of darkness scared her and the thought of spirits even more. What spirits did she mean? Marie tossed and turned, before finally getting up to look out the window. Her eyes moved along the shore, but she couldn't make out anything in the darkness.

She went over to the rocking chair in the room where a bisque doll dressed in a lace-trimmed pink gown sat. The doll had a head full of golden-brown rag curls and a beautifully painted face. Her grandmother had given it to her two years earlier before she had died. Marie cherished the doll and it was a source of comfort for her. Whenever she held it she was reminded of her grandmother's gentle, kind nature and it always soothed her. She picked up the doll and went back to her bed. She lay down once again with the doll under one arm and listened to the gentle rolling of the waves on the shore as she drifted off to sleep.

CHAPTER 4- A SONG ON THE WAVES

After dawn broke the next morning, Edward extinguished the light, put on his linen apron, and took to inspecting the third order Fresnel lens for damage as he did every day. He then picked up a piece of linen cloth and began cleaning the lens. It was a tedious task that had to be done daily. He was normally meticulous in the chore, but at the moment, he was mindlessly cleaning as his thoughts wandered. *Who are they? When will they strike again?* His anxiety had been heightened after learning that the three ships had been deliberately attacked and the crew of the last murdered. The thought of it had kept his mind preoccupied for the last two days. All of the incidents had occurred in Maine waters. Port DePaix had a large harbor where ships were always bringing in and taking away valuable cargo. It seemed that this crime ring was moving on from insurance fraud to piracy, and their last attack had only been a few miles away. Edward was worried that they might strike in the waters of Wawenock Point.

The sun was getting higher in the sky now and soon the lens would have to be covered again until nightfall. Edward's arms were becoming numb from the constant swiping motion and he had to stop for a moment before he started the process of polishing the glass with buff-skin. Afterward, he cleaned the oil lamp within the lens and all of its accessories. Once the cleaning was done and all the mechanical parts of the lantern appeared to be in order, he drew the curtains of the lantern room and covered the lens with a linen bag, both of which were done to prevent the sun from distorting the lens. Finally, he made notes in the watch book as to the condition of the lighthouse and the weather and recorded the hour his shift ended before signing off on it. He then descended the spiral stairs and walked out into the bright sunshine of a summer's morning.

Once outside, Edward turned to lock the door to the lighthouse. He was greeted by Margaret, who stood with a hand over her eyes to shade them from the rising sun. "There's a man here about some insurance business," she said.

Edward quirked an eyebrow. "Where is he?"

"In your office." She turned and quickly made her way back to the keeper's quarters with Edward following close behind.

He entered the office and found a man in his late twenties or so sitting there. "Good morning. How may I help you?" Edward greeted.

"Good morning, sir," the man said as he stood. "I'm Howard Martin. I am with the East Knox Insurance Company."

"I'm Edward Ashman. I'm the head keeper here." Edward held out his hand for the man to shake.

"I'm sorry to come unannounced," Martin said, shaking Edward's hand, "but I have some questions about the body that was found here the other day."

"I assume the police or the customs office informed your company about that?" Edward asked.

"They did," the man replied. "But I am investigating an incident involving one of our cargo ships that we believe the man may be connected to. The ship was called the *Josephine* and it was carrying a lot of valuable goods such as fine china and jewelry boxes. I just have some more questions that I need answered for my investigation."

"Of course." Edward gestured for the man to sit down. "Mr. Wilkins discussed the connection with us."

"I understand that you saw no suspicious activity the night before he was found," Martin stated as he took a seat. "I suppose you have seen nothing suspicious since?"

"No, I have not," Edward answered as he too took a seat.

"Did you find any articles such as personal effects or debris that day or since then that may be in relation to the man or the *Josephine*?"

"No, I'm afraid not, and if I did I would inform the police."

"Have you had any unusual visitors after the incident?"

"No, just you and a few police officers."

The man jotted down some notes in a pad he carried. "Would you mind showing me the exact location where the man was found?"

Edward hesitated for a moment before answering. "The police have photographs of the scene. Could you not ask them to see the pictures?" He wasn't sure why the man was making him go through all of this again when he had told the police everything he knew.

"Oh, I have, but there was something peculiar in one of the photographs and I'd like to see the scene for myself," Martin explained.

"Like what?"

"It's hard to explain, but I have an idea about something."

Edward didn't like how vague the man was being, but decided that perhaps Martin mistrusted the police and that there was no harm in letting him see where the body was found. Edward nodded and heeded the man's request. "Alright, I'll show you."

He stood and led the man outside to the rocks. "He was found about here." Edward pointed to the location where the body had been found. Martin looked around a bit before deciding to climb down the rocks. "I wouldn't do that; you could lose your footing," Edward warned.

"I will be fine," Martin said as he carefully made his way down the cliff. He kept looking around as if searching for something in particular. Once he seemed satisfied, he made his way back up the cliff.

"Well, doesn't look like any evidence got left behind," he announced as he wiped his hands off. "As you can understand, my company and I would like to find these criminals as soon as we can. We think they are behind two other shipping incidents as well. Those ships and their cargo were insured for thousands of dollars and my company is reluctant to pay money out on account of fraud. If there is anything you find or can think of to help, do not hesitate to contact me or my office." He quickly wrote down his name and office information on a page in his notepad and handed it to Edward.

"I will let you know if anything comes up," Edward assured him.

"Thank you. Good day to you, sir." Martin tipped his hat to Edward and quickly turned to leave.

"Good day!" Edward called after him, confused by his hurried retreat.

☙

Marie groggily awoke as the sun shone in through the windows. She sat up and looked to her side. Anna was already up and getting dressed. Marie reached down for her doll, but found it was not next to her. She looked under her sheets and then under the bed to no avail. The rocking chair was also empty.

"Did you take my doll?" she asked her sister.

"No." Anna looked up in confusion. Marie went over to her sister's side of the room and frantically looked under the covers and bed. "Stop it!" Anna yelled. "I didn't take your stupid doll!"

"Don't call her that!" Marie became angry. "Grandmother gave her to me before she passed."

"Yes, I know," Anna replied. "She didn't give me anything!"

"That's because you were still too little," Marie explained. "She was afraid that you wouldn't be mature enough to take care of something so precious."

"I most certainly would have been mature enough," Anna grunted as she crossed her arms.

"Don't be cross with me."

"Well, don't say I took your doll when I didn't."

"She couldn't have just disappeared," Marie said as she continued looking around the room.

"I don't know where she is, just don't blame me," Anna curtly told her sister before she turned and stalked out of the room.

Marie eventually gave up hope for finding the doll. She was completely puzzled as to where it could have gone. *Maybe Anna is really hiding it and just playing a trick on me because she's jealous*, she thought. Eventually, she decided to get dressed, putting on a white cotton dress with black piping. She started brushing her hair, but got caught on a snag. A back section of hair was twisted in a huge knot and she tried getting it out, but couldn't.

She got up and walked down the hall to her parents' bedroom. Her mother was sitting in the rocking chair holding Thomas. Marie was surprised to see her holding her little brother as Margaret was usually the one taking care of him. Frances didn't seem to notice her daughter walk into the room.

"Mother?" Marie sheepishly asked, still standing in the doorway.

Her mother looked up. "Oh, hello, dear, I didn't see you there."

"I have a knot in my hair," Marie said. "Can you get it out?"

"Yes, just let me put your brother in his crib." Frances gingerly got up, taking Thomas with her. After putting her son down, she walked over to Marie, who was standing in the center of the room. Frances stood behind her and Marie placed the brush in her mother's outstretched hand. The woman began to gently work out the knot in her daughter's locks.

She and her sister both had their mother's curly hair, except Marie's was a medium brunette shade like her father's while Anna had their mother's golden blonde hair. Marie also shared her father's honey brown eyes, while Anna had her mother's blue. After Frances worked the knot out, she continued to brush the rest of the girl's hair. Marie enjoyed being able to have this time in her mother's company. Ever since the baby was born, her mother had made herself scarce and both girls were being affected by her absence.

"Mother." Marie's voice quavered as she spoke. "Why are you so sad all the time?"

Frances slowed her brushing. "I…I don't know," she finally managed to say.

"Is it because of us?" Marie looked down, afraid of the answer.

"No, of course not." Frances was trying to think of a decent answer for her daughter, but couldn't. "It's just that taking care of Thomas is tiring."

"Isn't Margaret helping?" Marie started fidgeting with her hands.

"Yes, I owe her my gratitude." Her brushing had become focused in one area.

"Are…are you mad at Father?" The brush came to a halt. Marie's breath caught in her throat. She'd gone too far.

"You should not ask about things that have nothing to do with you." Her mother's words became harsh. "You are too young to be asking about such matters."

Marie looked down, her face turning red. "Forgive me," she muttered. "I should know my place."

"Indeed," was her mother's curt reply. Marie tried

hard to fight back the tears brimming in her eyes and her throat became constricted. Her mother gave her hair a few more strokes before she stopped. "Now go finish your chores."

"Yes, Mother," Marie said quietly, trying to keep her voice steady. As she left the room, the tears in her eyes flowed freely and she quietly wiped them away. Little did she know that her mother had just done the same.

~

Frances sat on the bed and sobbed. She still loved her husband, didn't she? Their marriage had grown strained over the past two months. She had been upset after her miscarriage, and although she felt better in time, she still carried the guilt and sadness with her and hid it from everyone, including her husband. Edward had been supportive, telling her that it happened to a lot of women, but she feared that he secretly blamed her, as she blamed herself, and she felt ashamed. She hadn't wanted to have another child, but he had convinced her by telling her that it could perhaps make up for the loss. After Thomas was born, she had only gotten worse. She was sad all the time and had lost interest in nearly everything. She felt overwhelmed and tired, especially when she was constantly worrying that something would happen to the baby or that she would do something wrong, despite her prior experience. Sometimes she was even afraid to sleep because of the fear that she would sleepwalk and hurt the baby or someone else. This anxiety usually caused her to shut down and not do anything, which on the outside made it look like she didn't want to take care of Thomas.

She didn't know what was wrong with her. She had been over the moon when Marie and Anna were born and was ready to take on being a parent, but this time she only felt irritation, even resentment, with motherhood and found herself projecting it at her husband a lot. When he tried to help or offered solutions, she would get annoyed and push him away.

With great trepidation she walked over to the crib in the corner of the room. There her baby son lay looking up at her with his big blue eyes. He was an adorable little one, and she wanted to love him, she really did, but she felt empty inside when it came to him. She hated herself for feeling that way. How could a mother not love her own child? But she just found herself unable to connect with him. Often when he cried, she didn't know how to soothe him and Margaret would have to take over. Even breastfeeding him seemed more difficult and painful than it had with her daughters. She felt like a failure as a mother.

"You deserve better than me," she said as she looked down at him. A teardrop fell on his forehead, causing him to flinch. She wiped it off and gently stroked his head.

"*Give him…*"

The harsh whisper made Frances stiffen as she froze with fear. It was the same eerie, gravelly voice again. She had first heard it only days after Thomas was born, and every day since then the voice made its presence known with more frequency.

"*Give him...*"

"No, stop it," she bit out. "Leave me alone."

"*Give him…*"

"Stop it! Stop it! Stop it!" she shouted, gripping the rails of the crib tightly. Why wouldn't the voice stop? "It's not real," she told herself, shaking her head furiously. Was she going insane? Was that why she was hearing the voice and felt nothing for her son?

Edward had taken her to the town's physician, Dr. Colson, who suggested she go see an alienist in the next town over. Dr. Colson had stated it seemed like she was suffering from puerperal insanity. She had been taken aback and didn't want to think it was possible. Edward had tried to persuade her to go see the alienist, but she was too afraid to. Now she thought that maybe she should as she seemed to only be getting worse.

When Edward came to the bedroom after his shift, Frances decided to bring up the subject again. "I was thinking…" she began shakily. "Maybe, maybe I should go see the alienist Dr. Colson referred. I mean it doesn't hurt to just talk to him, right?"

Edward raised his eyebrows in surprise, shocked that she had changed her mind. "Of course not," he replied. "He could very well provide you with the help you need."

She nodded. "I'm just afraid … what if he wants me to go to an asylum?"

"I don't think it will come to that," he tried to reassure her, but deep down he wasn't so certain. She continued to look down so he went over to her and took her face in his hands. "Take everything one step at a time," he told her. "Don't worry yourself sick."

He kissed her forehead and then embraced her. She breathed deeply as she rested her head on his shoulder, feeling a genuine affection for him that she hadn't in weeks.

❦

That night, Edward had the first shift. Before lighting up the lamp, he trimmed the wicks and made sure the oil level was correct. Then he released the weight of the clockwork mechanism to start the rotation of the Fresnel lens for the night. Afterward, he sat with his head against the wall of the watch room. He was trying his hardest to stay focused on the newspaper in front of him, but he kept closing his eyes and had to force himself to stay awake. The waves of the ocean could be heard off in the distance. The reverberation of the winds inside the tower was making an eerie noise that echoed throughout the structure. Edward felt himself beginning to doze off again when the faintest sound of singing caught his interest. He listened more intently. It was a woman's voice, almost operatic in its sound, but much gentler. There were no lyrics to the song, just the beautiful falling and rising of her voice.

Edward stood up from his seat and looked out through one of the small windows of the watch room. He didn't see anything out on the water. He then looked out along the coastline, now covered in darkness except when the ray from the light would shine over it. When the light hit the coast, he could have sworn he saw a woman walking on the small stretch of beach. He blinked and rubbed his eyes. He looked again when the light shined once more on the shore. There was no woman there. Confusion set in as he tried to figure out who was singing. He looked out one of the windows at the house, but there were no lights coming from any of the rooms. Still, could Margaret have been the one singing? He doubted it was Frances and the voice was too mature to be his daughters. He relaxed back into his seat and decided to close his eyes for awhile. Maybe it was floating across the water from the boardwalk or his tired mind was making something up. But he once again heard the beautiful singing, lulling him to sleep.

CHAPTER 5- THE TEMPTRESS

Margaret prepared breakfast for the family before Edward and Frances left for their appointment with the alienist. Frances only had a few nibbles of the food before excusing herself as she was too nervous to eat. The couple left and the girls went to start working on their chores. Margaret looked down at Frances's half eaten plate.

"What a waste," she grumbled.

She was going to save the leftovers for another day, but then Harry chimed in, "Give it to me. I'll finish it."

"You're going to get fat with all of this eating you've been doing," she scolded as she set the plate down in front of him.

"I need to build up my blubber for the winter," he joked.

"Your blubber," Margaret mimicked. "If you start looking like a whale I'm throwing your arse into the ocean."

"Do me a favor, please," Harry muttered.

Margaret rolled her eyes and went back to cleaning the plates. When she was finished she sat down at the table. "Harry, I'm tired," she sighed. "I'm getting too old to be taking care of someone else's children." She wiped a hand across her sweaty, freckled forehead.

"I know. I don't know what's wrong with that woman," he grumbled in agreement.

"I've had twice as many children as her and never acted like this," she stated. "You just have to pick yourself up by your bootstraps and do what you need to do."

"Well, not everyone can be as strong as you when it comes to children," he said. "Hell, I wanted to go insane half the time myself with all the damn kids we had."

"Well, it's your fault," she returned. "You got me pregnant with all of them."

"It's not my fault you breed faster than a rabbit in the middle of mating season...damn Irish loins of yours," he griped.

"Kiss me Irish arse."

"No, it might kill me." He shook his head, then reconsidered. "On second thought... turn around."

The request earned him a whack to the head.

～

Frances twisted a handkerchief in her hands as she waited for Dr. Neumann to take her into his office. The alienist's place of work was well furnished and Edward couldn't help but wonder about the cost of this appointment. He placed his hand on top of his wife's to still her fidgeting and to reassure her. The doctor came out a moment after his previous patient left and called for the couple to come into the office.

Dr. Neumann, a tall, broad-shouldered man in his late forties, held out his hand in greeting. "Mr. Ashman, Mrs. Ashman, pleased to meet you," he said. "Please take a seat." He gestured to two chairs in the room.

"Thank you," Frances said quietly as she sat down and Edward followed suit.

Dr. Neumann sat down in a chair opposite them. "So, Mrs. Ashman, I understand you have been suffering quite a bit after the birth of your last child. Tell me what you have been experiencing."

She breathed deeply and looked at Edward, who nodded for her to continue. "I… well…I cry a lot," she said, finding it difficult to speak about this.

"What makes you cry?" Dr. Neumann asked.

"I don't know; it's a lot of things," she explained. "Sometimes it's because I feel overwhelmed and other times because I just feel so hopeless."

"Do you feel overburdened by taking care of your family?" he asked as he made a note on his writing pad.

"I do, but I don't understand why. I've never felt that way in the past when I had my daughters."

"How many children do you have?"

"I have three: two girls and now a son."

"Was there anything difficult about this past birth? Any trouble with the delivery or fever afterward?" he asked.

"No, everything went fine and no fever."

"She did have a miscarriage about two years ago," Edward chimed in.

"Well, that could certainly be a contributing

factor, especially if it made you more anxious during this pregnancy," he stated. "When did you start feeling this way?"

"Maybe about a week or so after my son was born."

"That is typical for a lot of women," he remarked. "How many months old is your son now?"

"Two months."

"So this has been going on for some time," he commented as he stood. "If you wouldn't mind standing for a moment, I'd like to take a quick look at your physical state."

She did so and he came up to her to feel her forehead. "Skin is a bit cold," he remarked. Then he took her wrist to feel her pulse. "Pulse is slow. Open your mouth, please." She felt awkward as she stood there mouth agape while he looked. "Tongue is pale and indented." He then pressed on her lower abdomen. "Does that hurt at all?"

"No," she responded flatly, hoping this exam would end soon.

The doctor seemed to read her mind as he said, "You may sit now." He returned to his chair and made some more notes as Edward and Frances exchanged glances. "Well, your physical state appears to align with a depressive state. How have you been sleeping?" he inquired, noticing her dull eyes and the dark circles under them.

"Not very well," she noted. "Sometimes I cannot even sleep when the baby is sleeping."

He nodded as he continued to jot his notes. "Your face is also a bit pale and thin. I am assuming your appetite is lacking as well?"

Frances just nodded so Edward stated, "She

doesn't eat as much as she used to."

"But does she have an active aversion to food?" He turned his attention to Edward. Noticing the other man's confused face, Neumann clarified his statement. "What I mean is does she consistently refuse food to the point where she must be forced to eat."

"No, at least, not that I am aware."

Frances spoke up. "It is not that I don't want to eat, it is just that I often don't feel hungry or my stomach is too uneasy to eat."

He looked at Edward. "How has she behaved toward you? Any irritability or violence?"

"Well, sometimes she gets angry at me and we argue, but no violence."

"And how well does she keep the household?"

"Uhm, well… she tries to do her usual cleaning and cooking, but she often has someone else take up a lot of the chores she finds herself incapable of performing." He chose his words carefully, not wanting to make his wife look lazy in front of the doctor.

Dr. Neumann looked back at Frances. "Aside from anything that would cause physical strain, what is preventing you from doing your normal duties?"

The question felt like a punch to the gut. It reminded her of just how weak she felt. She sniffled and had difficulty voicing her response. "I don't know. Sometimes I start to get so worried that I might make a mistake or I just start to feel like I have so much to do that I… I just cannot function and I isolate myself from everyone and everything. It's like I'm hiding."

She looked down as she tried to hide the tears at

the edges of her eyes. Neumann twirled one of the ends of his thick handlebar mustache as he stared at her in contemplation. "When you say you are afraid of making a mistake, are you afraid you might hurt your children or husband?" he finally asked.

The tears fell from her eyes as she nodded. "I don't know why I'm so afraid I'll hurt the baby. I already have two children and taking care of this one should be so easy, but I worry all the time that I might drop him or something else. I don't trust myself."

Edward was shocked to hear this from her. Was this why she always seemed reluctant to take care of Thomas? She had no problems when taking care of the girls in the past and had been excellent with rearing them, so it hurt him to see that she no longer had confidence in her own abilities as a mother.

"Frances, you aren't going to hurt him," Edward said gently as he squeezed her hand, which was currently clutching her handkerchief tightly. "Think about how you were when the girls were born. You never hurt them."

"I know, but this time it feels so different," she said sadly.

"Forgive me for asking, but I need to." They both looked up at Dr. Neumann. "Do you ever have any thoughts or desires of willingly hurting your child?"

She shook her head forcefully. "No, of course not."

"That is good. And one final question: do you ever hear or see anything out of the ordinary?"

Frances swallowed hard. She hesitated for a second before she answered, "No." She wondered if it was enough of a pause for the doctor to know she was lying.

He simply nodded before writing down some more notes and then he gave his diagnosis. "Well, Mrs. Ashman, it appears that you have puerperal insanity in its melancholic form," he declared.

"So I am crazy?" she blurted out.

He chuckled. "I wouldn't quite put it that way. A lot of women suffer from this insanity after giving birth. And it usually appears more in women who have had male children and multiple births. Is there anyone in your family who has suffered from insanity?"

She shook her head. "Not that I know of."

"So given the lack of a hereditary link and complications with the birth, I think yours may have come on from the previous miscarriage and general fear and anxiety with this pregnancy and child," he explained. "I am going to prescribe a treatment regimen for you. I see more mania cases with this type of insanity, but the treatment is relatively the same. I want you to get plenty of rest and your bedroom should be well ventilated and lit. And in your case, I think confining yourself to your room for extended periods to take time away from chores and the baby would do you good. I will also give you a prescription for chloral. This will help you sleep. You also need to eat more. A good diet should consist of broths, milk, eggs, and starchy foods. I would also advise you to take warm baths as they are often helpful. When your condition allows you, you must take outdoor exercise as well."

Although Frances was trying to take in everything he was saying, she realized that his treatment plan was meant to be done at home. "So you aren't sending me to an asylum?"

"On no, I don't think there is a need for that at this stage," he reassured her.

She let out a tiny smile in relief. "That's good."

"Do you think you can do all these things for me?" he asked.

"Yes, sir," she responded quickly.

"Good, then I would like to see you in another two weeks to see how you are progressing."

"Very well." Frances stood up hurriedly. "Thank you so much for your help."

"Not at all." He smiled. He stopped Edward as he was about to leave. "Mr. Ashman, if I could speak to you for a moment while you wait outside, Mrs. Ashman."

Edward nodded at Frances, who closed the door behind her. Dr. Neumann stood and came closer to Edward. "I did not want to say this in front of your wife as I did not want to upset her further," he stated. "You will need to keep a close eye on your wife until she improves. With mental depression cases, there are often tendencies to suicide or violence. Needless to say, I would keep anything that can be used as a weapon away from her."

Edward swallowed hard. "Do you think she's that bad?"

"Well, some of her statements, such as she feels hopeless and doesn't trust herself, are concerning, not to mention her fears that she might hurt the baby."

Edward sighed. The possibilities of her ending her own life or hurting the baby were scary thoughts that he always kept hidden in the back of his mind and it was jarring to hear another person acknowledge the fear he had. "What can I do to help her, aside from making sure that she follows your treatment regimen?"

"Just give her kindness and reassurance," Dr. Neumann stated. "This can be one of the most difficult times in a woman's life; she will need all the support she can get."

Edward nodded. "What is her chance for recovery?"

"I think it is a bit too early to tell. Full recovery isn't usually reached until menstruation returns to normal anyway. For now we will see how she progresses with the treatment," he explained. "But of course, if she does not recover and gets worse, there is also the hospital in Augusta."

Edward shook his head. "I don't want to send her there and I know she really doesn't want to go."

"Let's hope it does not come to that, but if it does, I can assure you the staff there are very good. I know the superintendent personally and he is a very caring physician." The doctor's words didn't do much to soothe Edward. He thanked the doctor for his time and he and Frances made their way home.

❧

Hanlon woke up later than he had planned. The woman across his chest was still dead asleep. The two of them drank far too much last night. He rubbed his eyes as the light came in through the windows. His head was spinning and he could feel a terrible headache coming on. Gently, he pushed the woman off of him, trying not to wake her. He swung his legs over one side of the bed and rested his elbows on his knees. He put his head in his hands, slowly getting adjusted to his surroundings. When he felt the dizziness wane, he got up and picked his clothes up off the floor. He was dressing when the woman on the bed stirred.

"Mmmm, leaving me so soon?" she murmured as she woke.

"Sorry, Lily, but I'm late for work as is," he replied. "And I still have to go home and change."

"You should just keep an extra pair of clothes here," she suggested.

"And risk your husband finding them?" He raised an eyebrow.

Lily was the wife of one of Port DePaix's wealthier residents, Herbert Adler. She and Hanlon had begun their affair a few months ago, sneaking around whenever they could. Now, Adler was away for a few days on some business or other so it had been the perfect chance for them to have some fun.

"Fair enough," she agreed, then let out a groan. "My head feels like it's going to burst."

"Better get back to sleep then," Hanlon said as he pulled on his suit jacket. Then he sat on the bed to put his shoes and socks on.

Lily wrapped her arms around him. "I wish you didn't have to go," she whispered.

"Me neither, but I have a job to do," he explained. "And you don't want the neighbors growing suspicious."

"What excuse are you going to give your boss?"

He shrugged. "Stomachache, I suppose. It wouldn't be far from the truth."

With that he kissed her goodbye and then poked his head out the door to see if the maid was around before quietly making his way downstairs. He left out the back door to avoid the sight of any nosy neighbors. With hurried steps, he made his way across town back to his own home. It was a small house with a plain façade and a plain interior. Sighing as he looked around at his home, he made his way up to the bedroom to change. He lived comfortably enough, but he wanted more. He had grown up poor and resolved to himself that he would never be forced to go hungry or wear old holey clothing again. That's why he tried to dress impressively and mingle with those above his class, using his position in the police force to gain entry into their world. And when he met Lily, a young woman who was the third wife of a decrepit, rich man, he took the chance to relieve her of her boredom. Hanlon was a bachelor and was playing the long game, waiting for the old man to die so he could marry his wealthy widow.

Perhaps this time he had reached too far. He had gotten too greedy and not only was he taking advantage of a lonely woman, but he was risking ruining them both should anyone discover the affair. Of course, it would be the only spot on his otherwise flawless reputation, but it could well be something impossible for him to come back from. Shaking the thoughts from his head, he made his way to the police station. He passed by officers and greeted them curtly. Just as he turned the corner, he came face to face with his boss, Chief David Bouchard.

"Hanlon," the man stated firmly. "Where have you been? You look like hell."

"I apologize for my tardiness," he answered. "My stomach was upset all night. Must have been something I ate."

Bouchard gave him a disbelieving look. "Or

something you drank." He never missed the opportunity to take a jab at Hanlon's Irish heritage. Bouchard held up a piece of paper. "Anyway, just got this in this morning," he announced. On the paper were drawings of three men with a reward posted at the bottom. "All the local police departments were given copies. According to the captain of the lumber ship, this is what the three men who he signed on looked like as best he could recall."

"So that man they found with his throat cut wasn't one of them?" Hanlon asked, studying the drawings.

"Well, therein is where the controversy lies," Bouchard stated. "The captain said he sort of looked like one of the three men he signed on, but he wasn't sure, especially with the rotting from being out in the elements. Then I had some of the men here swearing it's the corpse of Timothy Ross. He's a repeat offender who's gotten into trouble around town before. But when we asked his mother to look at the body down at the morgue, she swore to Heaven it wasn't her son."

"Well, if he's been in and out of prison, when's the last time she's seen him?"

"That's a good question, so that's why I asked his brother to view the body," Bouchard answered. "He's coming down from Bangor either tonight or tomorrow."

"So until we can get confirmation of the man's identity, it's possible all three of the criminals could still be out there?"

"Yes, so take a good look at these men." Bouchard tapped the paper for emphasis. "And one more thing, I want you to look through all of your records. See if there are any inconsistencies or anything suspicious."

"Why, sir?" Hanlon looked at his superior cautiously.

"I think someone in this office may be cooperating with these criminals."

"Has something come up?"

"Well, as soon as it appeared that there was insurance fraud going on, the owner of the *Josephine* disappeared," Bouchard explained. "He lived right here in Port DePaix, in one of the mansions on the east side of town, and when I sent someone to go question him, he was gone. No one knows where he went. And I know the papers haven't said anything about the insurance fraud yet."

"So someone in this department must have told him," Hanlon finished for him. *Someone like you maybe?* Hanlon thought, remembering how his boss had apparently spoken to Wilkins about the previous crimes.

"Exactly." The chief nodded. "So keep your eyes and ears open."

"Of course, sir," Hanlon assured him and went to sit at his desk. He looked around at his coworkers, suddenly wary of them all.

☙

Night had fallen over the coast once again and Edward had resumed his position in the watch room. He was reading his evening paper, stopping to look out the window every now and again. Unsurprisingly, the RC *Gresham*, one of the Revenue Cutter Service's ships, was slowly sailing by, making its rounds of patrolling the northeast coast of the country. Thankfully, Edward had yet to see any trouble out on the sea. He quietly flipped through the pages in the newspaper. The crinkling of the paper was the only noise in the room next to Harry's snoring. The older man decided to take his rest in the watch room instead of his bed before beginning his own shift, probably to avoid his wife. The man would sleep all day if he could. He was in his early sixties and from what he had told Edward, he didn't have an easy life. He'd grown up poor with an abusive father and a mother who died young. He went on to serve in the Navy during the Civil War and had come close to death several times. Then he met Margaret and she'd given him a whole brood of children to provide for. Life had exhausted him. Edward sometimes wished he didn't sleep so much though. These nighttime shifts could be lonely and it would be nice to talk to someone. The man's wisdom, gained through years of living, would be a comfort.

Edward returned his attention to his newspaper. He was currently interested in a story about the Navesink Twin Lights in New Jersey. A power plant was built beside the lighthouse to generate electricity and one of the towers there was electrified. In place of an oil lamp, an electric arc lamp was installed in the lighthouse and it was so bright, it caused the other tower to be decommissioned. This news made Edward wonder what would happen if all the lighthouses in the country were eventually electrified. Would it cause more lighthouses to be decommissioned if they were no longer needed? What would happen to him and the other keepers?

When his eyes grew tired, he decided to stop

reading and put his head against the wall. He closed his eyes, lost in thought. Then he heard it again, the singing from the night before. It was louder this time and more haunting. He quickly got up and looked out at the shore. He could see a small light coming from the beach. When the beacon shined there he could see the outline of a woman and a small fire on the beach. His heart began to beat faster and his breath caught. He waited for the light to shine again. This time, the woman was still there.

He stopped for a minute, thinking what to do. His thoughts immediately went to the shipwreckers. What if this was part of their next plot to attack a ship? What if this woman made the fire to trick ships into thinking it was a distress call? It was possible that when the crews were distracted by this supposed woman in need, the criminals made their move. For a moment he became frozen by his frantic thoughts, but then he tried to think more rationally. The ships' crews would see that there was a lighthouse right there; the woman could just go to them instead of flagging down a ship. That would be the rational way of thinking, wouldn't it? He also realized that this woman could very well be in danger if she in fact had nothing to do with the criminals. He was supposed to help those in need, though why someone in need would be singing that way, he couldn't comprehend.

He got up and walked over to Harry. "Harry." He tried to nudge the man awake. "Harry!"

The man grumbled briefly, but wouldn't wake. Shaking his head, Edward reluctantly grabbed the nearest lantern and made for the stairs. He looked around the bottom floor for anything he could possibly use as a weapon. He didn't see anything, but then remembered he kept a pocket knife on him. He would use it if the need arrived. He walked out of the tower, closing the door behind him. The singing resounded in his ears and he felt the uncontrollable urge to get closer to the source of the sound, forgoing any other safety precautions.

It was like his body had a mind of its own, forcing him to keep walking toward the shore. In the back of his mind, he knew this wasn't safe, but the sound of this woman's beautiful singing was too tempting. He had to see the woman behind the voice, reason and safety be damned. As he moved closer to the beach, he could see the fire. The woman was circling the flames, swaying her body in rhythm to her song. He clumsily made his way down the slope of rocks to the beach. His walking slowed as he moved closer to her, awestruck.

> *Come to thee,*
> *Come and see,*
> *All you desire,*
> *In the flames of the fire,*
> *The world I give in bliss,*
> *But do take heed,*
> *For wishes go amiss,*
> *And ruin proceeds.*

Her song was enchanting and terrifying all at once. She had yet to face him, but he could tell that she knew he was there. He walked a bit closer. In the firelight he could just make out her stunning features. She had long wavy brown hair that reached her calves, but didn't hide her soft curves. Her skin was tanned and it glowed in the firelight. She finally caught his gaze, looking over her shoulder. Her shining violet eyes were her most distinguishing feature. She slowly walked toward him, smiling seductively, her song no longer pouring from her throat.

"Uh…miss…" He was trying his hardest to put coherent sentences together. "Are you…are you hurt? Do you need help?"

"I've been waiting for you," she said, her smile growing, "I'm glad you finally came." She ran a hand down her chest, pulling the top of her dress down, revealing more cleavage. He averted his eyes, trying not to look at her scantily clad figure. Her dress was sleeveless and ended just below her knees. It almost looked like a bunch of rags lazily draped over her body. It was translucent and helped to accentuate her curves; scandalous indeed.

"I don't know what you mean." Edward was growing uncomfortable. His senses were beginning to return now that she had stopped singing.

"I called to you last night." Her voice was breathy and silky. "Did you not hear?"

"I heard you singing, but I didn't think anything of it," he said, his suspicion growing. "How did you end up here?"

"I come to this place a lot," she said, staring at him intently. "It's practically my home." She walked closer to him and he instinctively took a step back. "Oh, come now, don't be afraid of me."

"You shouldn't be here," he said, his voice shaking slightly. "It's not safe out here in the middle of the night."

"Don't worry about me; I can take care of myself." She took another step closer. "I can take care of you too." She moved forward and placed a kiss on the corner of his mouth.

He immediately pushed her back and a hint of anger flickered across her face. "What are you doing?" His reason had returned.

"I'm giving you what you need, since your wife will not." A devilish grin appeared on her lips.

"I'm a happily married man, I don't need you," he spat.

"Lies," she whispered, her violet eyes boring into him. "Your wife is miserable and that makes you miserable."

"You don't know what you're talking about." His anger and fear were rising. "You don't know anything about me."

"Oh, I know." She began circling him, then came closer to him and whispered in his ear, "Your distress is radiating off you." She came closer to his face again, trying once more for a kiss. He reached for the knife in his pocket. "Do you really think that knife can stop me?"

He just stared at her, his eyes growing large. *How could she have known that?* He could see now that her eyes were glowing and it terrified him. "What...what are you?" he managed to whisper.

She snickered. "If you want to know what I am, I suggest you read up on your mythology. Come back to me when you do." She turned from him then and sashayed back to the fire.

He stood for another moment, frozen in place. She turned back to him. "Go," she said more sternly and her gaze became icy. She turned from him again and hummed a one-note tune. As if by another force, he turned to go and found his feet moving of their own accord. He looked back at her once more, part of him wanting to confront her further. She stood facing the fire, no longer acknowledging him. Something was urging him to continue on, though, and his heart was racing the entire way back to the lighthouse. Oddly, when he looked out the windows, she was gone and so was the fire on the beach. He shook his head, not quite comprehending what had just happened, but he couldn't think of anything but the woman the rest of the night. Her words and her face haunted him. He knew he would find it hard to sleep when morning came.

CHAPTER 6- HORROR AT SEA

Edward walked into the keeper's quarters the next morning after finishing his shift. The encounter with the strange woman last night had left him shaken and he was glad to have not seen her when the sun rose. He walked into the bedroom and was pleased to see Frances sleeping soundly for once, the chloral seeming to help. A light breeze was blowing through the open window and sunlight was pouring in, just as the doctor had advised. He went over to the crib, where he found Thomas fast asleep too. He stroked the light wisps of hair on his son's head, gently so as not to wake him. He took off his navy uniform and quietly slipped into bed. Unfortunately, the action stirred Frances in her sleep and her eyes fluttered open.

"Edward," she mumbled.

"Sorry, I didn't mean to wake you," he apologized.

"It's alright. I actually got a full night's rest for once," she reassured him.

"That's good, you need it."

She nodded. "I should make breakfast before the girls get up. Thomas is still sleeping, right?"

"Yes, but make sure you eat too."

"I know." She made to get up, but he stopped her and pulled her close.

"Stay with me for a bit," he murmured as he snuggled up to her. "I feel like I hardly see you anymore."

"Alright." She turned to face him and got closer to him. She noticed the consternation on his face. "Edward, what's the matter? Something seems to be troubling you."

He shook his head, deciding not to tell her about his strange encounter last night. "Just tired is all."

"You need to get more sleep, too," she said, then added guiltily, "I know I'm partly to blame."

"Shhh." He nuzzled his nose in her hair. "It's not your fault."

"Edward, can I be honest with you?" Her voice was small.

"Of course." He nodded as his eyes drooped.

"I don't think this treatment is going to work," she said despondently.

"How can you tell, you just started it." He was perplexed.

She shrugged. "I just don't see how anything he told me to do is that different from what I do regularly besides getting more sleep."

"You really need to stop thinking so negatively," he said quietly. "It will only make it worse."

"Nothing could make this worse," she said, her voice quivering.

"Well, when you talk like that…"

Her shoulders sank and she turned away from him. He could tell, however, it was just her attempt to hide her tears. "I feel like I'm crumbling apart. I don't want to die, but sometimes I think if I did… it would be a relief." Her voice was barely above a whisper.

"How could you say that?" He was taken aback.

"I hate this, I hate it so much, I hate myself." She started to sob.

"Don't say that." He attempted to turn her rigid body back toward him. "You don't hate yourself and you're going to get through this."

She let herself be turned around. "I don't know… I don't know." Her face was tear-stained and red.

He pulled her close. "Listen to me. Stop this; you will get better."

She breathed shakily before she asked very quietly, almost in a whisper, "Do you still love me?"

"What kind of question is that? Of course I do." She buried her face in his chest and he held her until he fell asleep.

☙

Marie was finishing up dusting the furniture when Anna came running into their bedroom. She was breathing heavy.

"What are you running for?" Marie stopped what she was doing to stare at her little sister.

"I found it!" she cried, a smile lighting up her face. "The cave!"

Marie sighed deeply. "I told you there's no cave around here! You shouldn't pay any mind to the stories Peggy tells you."

"But it's true!" Anna cried back. "There really is a

cave! It's on the side of the rocks behind the lighthouse!"

Marie just stared at her sister, annoyed. "I don't have time for your games."

But Anna would not be swayed. "You need to come see it for yourself." She walked over to Marie and pulled her hand.

"No, I'm not going." Marie tried pulling back. "I have a lot to do here!"

"Please come!" Anna pleaded with her. "I don't want to go in there by myself!"

"Anna." Marie's tone became more serious, very much like her father's would.

"Marie, please." Anna looked up at her, her eyes showing desperation. "I'm not lying, I swear. Please come!"

Marie looked at her, considering for a moment. "Fine," she finally decided. "But if you're lying I'm telling Father you were playing by the rocks again."

The younger girl became more excited and pulled the older girl out of the room. They walked outside, passing the lighthouse and the storage shed, making their way to the far side of the cliff. The girls carefully maneuvered their way over the large rocks. Anna led them to a place where the rocks sloped outward, creating something of a ledge to walk on. Moving around a few more rocks, the girls reached a space between two large rocks that had a deep tunnel-like entrance.

Marie's eyes grew wide in surprise. "Well, I never would have thought…"

"I told you! I moved that other rock out of the way earlier," Anna said, pointing to another large, flat rock that lay in front of the tunnel entrance. "And there was an opening here to the cave."

"How could you move that rock all by yourself?" Marie asked.

"It wasn't that heavy… and I might have just pushed it over." Anna was small enough to walk into the cave straight on and did so. "Come on!"

"I don't think we should be going in here." Marie was hesitant. "It's dark and we don't know what's in there."

"It's not that dark. Come on already." Anna moved further into the cave.

If Anna wasn't her sister, Marie wouldn't have cared what trouble the girl got into. But as it was, Marie reluctantly followed, having to duck a bit and pull her shoulders in as she went. Once she got past the narrow opening, Marie was able to stretch to her full height as the cave interior widened. It was dim inside and it took a moment for one's eyes to adjust to the change in light. As Marie followed Anna, it was impossible to tell how far back the cave went.

"How did you even find this place?" Marie found the whole situation odd.

"I was just walking over here and it sounded like wind," she explained. "Then I felt a breeze by one of the rocks. I pushed it and saw that there was a whole cave behind it!"

"I really think we should turn back." Marie was becoming more nervous.

"Look!" Anna suddenly stopped in front of a carved-out place in the side of the cave. "There's all sorts of things down here!"

Marie went over to where she was and looked inside the depression. She was surprised at everything that was there. There were all types of bottles. Some were round, some small, some large, some thin and long. They came in all sorts of blues and greens and browns. Next to them was a large pile of coins. Many looked modern, but some looked completely foreign to Marie, even ancient in their appearance. Next to them was a large mason jar filled with different kinds of seashells. Another mason jar was filled with buttons. What interested Marie the most was how neatly laid out it all was. But then she realized whoever put all of this here might still be nearby.

"We should leave before whoever put this here comes back," she hurriedly told her sister.

Anna was busy looking at some of the coins. "I doubt they'll be here for awhile," she said. "They can't live down here."

Marie's heart was racing, but then she spied something familiar out of the corner of her eye. "My doll!" she cried. "I knew it! You took her and put her here!"

Anna looked up in complete surprise. "How could I have put her here when I just found the cave this morning and she's been gone for days!" she defended herself. "I didn't even see her there!"

"You're lying!" Marie was angry now. "I bet you put all of these things here!"

"I didn't!" Anna yelled. "How could I have gotten all of this stuff without you seeing!"

"It's not like I see you every second of every day, you would have had plenty of time to do it," Marie said "And besides, if you didn't put her here, who did? I doubt Peggy or Mother or Father would have!"

"But I swear I didn't!" Anna cried.

"I'm telling Mother about this!" Marie grabbed her doll and began to walk back to the house.

"No, don't!" Anna started following, but then a hand on her arm stopped her.

"Don't worry about her," a soft voice said beside her. "I have more to show you."

Anna stopped and turned to see the figure of a little boy. She nodded and followed him back into the cave.

☙

Edward resumed his position in the watch room that night. The evening's paper contained sketches of the suspected shipwreckers. The images were too vague in Edward's opinion to be able to identify the men if he ran into them on the street and the descriptions of them weren't much better. The only thing that stood out was that one of them had a scar on his left cheek. Growing tired of the headlines, he picked up his daughter's copy of *Bulfinch's Mythology: The Age of Fable* and began reading it. He had taken it from Marie's night table when she had been out of the house. He was questioning his mental state right now. Was he honestly supposed to believe the woman from last night was someone out of mythology? But then how could she have known about Frances and his knife? And her singing had drawn him in, pulling him to her against his will.

He skimmed the pages in the book, looking for something that fit her features. She didn't fit the descriptions of any of the goddesses in the book. It wasn't until he got to the section on Ulysses that he finally started to find something familiar. He first read the section on Circe. Was the woman some sort of sorceress with the powers to turn men into beasts?

There was a mention of singing under that section and Circe's powers of enchanting men would fit the woman. Then he got to the next section: the sirens. They were creatures who drew sailors to their deaths with their beautiful songs.

He laughed to himself. Was he really going to believe that this woman was a siren? Some ancient creature? He just shook his head. Maybe he hadn't seen her at all. Maybe she was just a dream; something conjured up by his mind from all the stress he had been under lately. But he knew very well that he had been awake last night and that the woman was indeed real. He just could not accept that she was a magical creature. It would be mad to believe so.

Edward put the book down and looked out the window. There was no sign of the siren and nothing out on the water but gentle waves. He also didn't hear any singing tonight. Seeing that all was quiet, he resumed reading the book. A half hour passed without incident, and then a loud boom made Edward bolt upright.

"The hell was that!" he exclaimed.

He looked out the window and saw a bright light in the middle of the open sea. It took him a second to realize that it was a ship on fire. He grabbed the binoculars to try and get a closer look. He could have sworn he saw a man jump into the water. Turning quickly, he raced down the lighthouse steps and outside. He could hear the shouts of men coming from the water.

"Ed!" He turned to see Harry coming out of the keeper's quarters. "What happened out here? I heard a loud bang!"

"I'm not sure!" Edward yelled back. "I heard it

too and next thing I know there's a ship on fire!"

"I'll go into town and get help! Maybe there's a ship in the harbor that can help!" Harry announced.

Then Edward heard a scream come from behind him. He turned to see the flames had grown in intensity. He swallowed hard, knowing what that meant. "Harry, I don't know if those men will be able to wait for help to arrive," he said.

"You think we should get out there?" Harry asked as he looked at the burning ship.

"Yes," Edward answered. "I'll send up a flare though just in case."

Edward ran to the storage shed and with as much dexterity as he could muster while trying to hurry, he pulled out a flare. Once outside, he set it up near the edge of the rocks and lit it. He watched as it shot up into the sky, sending brilliant sparks out into the black night. Edward was hoping the *Gresham* or another well-equipped ship wasn't too far away and would be able to come to their aid. Something in his gut told him this wasn't the usual shipping accident.

He and Harry wasted no more time and made their way past the lighthouse and over to the rocks. There was a small ramp that ran over the cliff and a peapod-style rowboat was kept tied to it. The two men climbed in and Harry untied the rope. With vigor, they rowed to the flaming ship.

As they got closer they could see a gaping hole in the hull of the ship. The heat coming from the flames was unbearable in the July night. The light from the fire allowed them to make out the name of ship, the *Cornelius Wade*, painted on her side. There was debris from the ship scattered throughout the sea. The *Wade* was taking on water and a lot of the crew members had jumped into the ocean. A small group of them were still on the ship trying to rig up a hose to put out the fire, which had now spread to the wooden main deck. When the men in the water saw the boat from the lighthouse coming their way, they scrambled toward it.

"What happened?" Edward called out as they reached the first man.

The man grabbed Edward's offered arm and answered. "There was an explosion, but I don't know how it happened! I saw the fire and jumped ship."

"Coal fire probably!" another man that Harry was helping aboard shouted in return.

"No way it would cause that much damage," the first man disagreed.

"Help!" The men turned to see another man clambering around furiously, trying to keep his head above water. They rowed toward him and Harry got wet reaching down to grab him. Clearly not adept at swimming or floating, the man was so frantic he nearly pulled Harry down with him. With a little help from the other men, Harry managed to pull the man aboard.

As they made their way through the water, they helped two more men onto the boat. Carefully, they rowed closer to the ship. Two men were still in the water crying out in pain as they held onto pieces of debris to keep afloat. When Edward and Harry pulled them out of the water, the extent of the damage was plain to see. One of the men's entire left side was torn up from the explosion. He was covered in blood and screamed when he was pulled aboard. The other was badly burned on his face and right arm.

Suddenly, there was a popping sound and Edward

looked up just in time to see a piece of hot metal go whizzing past his head. Apparently, whatever had caused the explosion wasn't quite finished yet.

"We need to get out of the way, *now*!" Edward ordered and he quickly started to move the rowboat away from the ship.

Meanwhile on deck, the other crew members gave up trying to use the hose as the fire continued to grow and the ship took on more water. They instead made for the ship's lifeboat while an older, stocky man remained on deck.

"I have to see who's still below!" he shouted. "I have to go back for them!"

"Captain, it's an inferno!" another man called back. "You can't get down there!"

The captain ignored him and made his way below deck through a hatch on the opposite side of the flames. "What do we do?" one of the men in the lifeboat asked.

"Dammit! Let me go get him!" The first man climbed out of the lifeboat and went after the captain.

After only a few seconds the man and the captain were both back on deck and running to the lifeboat. Their faces were blackened from coal dust and smoke and both were coughing profusely. When they both had boarded the lifeboat, the captain commanded, "Lower her!" He then proceeded to have a coughing fit as the lifeboat reached the water. Edward and Harry rowed the peapod over to the *Wade*'s lifeboat.

"You're the captain?" Edward asked, looking at the older man.

"I am. Captain Clarence Morris," he choked out.

"How many were aboard, Captain?" Edward inquired.

"I had twenty-one aboard, including myself," he answered and counted the men in the two boats. "I'm missing seven!" he called out.

"Where's John?"

Then one of them declared, "Paul is missing!"

"And Ernest!"

"What about Oliver and Roy?"

"Dan! Louis! Are you out there?"

They called out the names of the seven men who were missing in case they were still in the water, but there was no response. Then someone exclaimed, "Something's floating over there!"

They rowed closer to the object, only to see that it was a human form. One of the men reached out and pulled him close. "It's Paul..." was the soft call. The men in the lifeboat pulled the corpse aboard. The back of his body was torn up badly. They rowed around the burning ship some more, but found no one floating amongst the debris.

"The others... they're still on the ship," the captain solemnly announced.

"Christ...torn to pieces," one of the men next to Harry murmured.

"Or burned to death," another said.

The men watched in silence as the fire continued and caused the iron side of the ship to warp from the heat. Another popping sound was heard and the men knew that was the signal to get going. The two boats made their way back to shore just as another bang from the ship filled the air. The men in both boats headed up the ramp, with the crew carrying the injured and Paul. As they walked up to the keeper's quarters, Margaret and Frances were standing there in their nightgowns and robes.

"What in God's name happened out there?" Margaret asked.

"A ship was passing by when there was an explosion," Edward explained. "The men will stay in the parlor for now. Some of them need medical attention."

"I'll get the supplies." Margaret turned and hurried back into the house.

"You're not hurt, are you?" Frances asked.

"No, I'm fine, just a bit startled is all," Edward answered.

"I'm sure," Frances said. "Bring them inside. I will go help Margaret."

Edward and Harry ushered the men into the parlor. The two women helped to clean and dress the wounds of the injured as best they could. Many of the men had burns, some more mild than others, and were grimacing in pain as the women treated their scorched flesh. The uninjured men wrapped Paul's body up in a sheet and placed it in the corner of the room.

"I'll go to the police station," Edward told Harry. "They can send an ambulance."

As he was making his way out the door, he saw Marie and Anna standing on the stairs.

"Papa, what happened?" Anna asked. "We saw the fire."

"There was an accident," he said. "Some of the men on the boat got injured."

"Is there anything we can do to help?" Marie asked.

"Maybe you can go get the men some coffee or water."

The girls nodded and went into the kitchen. They

brought out refreshments for the men and blankets for those who were wet from being in the water. Several minutes later, Edward came back with multiple policemen. The most severely injured men were taken by ambulance to the nearest hospital and Paul was taken away by the coroner. The police asked the men several questions about what had happened to their ship, but no one was really able to give an explanation. Hanlon arrived with the police and asked questions of the men as well.

"Were there any signs of fire before the explosion?" Hanlon asked.

"I went to check on the temperature of the coal bunkers a few hours before the explosion," the ship's engineer explained. "One near where the explosion occurred rated a higher temperature than the others, but I felt no excessive heat or smelled burning coal or saw any smoke."

"So is it possible that a coal fire had started between when you checked on the bunkers and when the explosion occurred?" Hanlon inquired further.

"Of course," the engineer answered. "But coal fires are slow burning. It wouldn't have caused that kind of explosion in so short a time."

"Is it possible it was one of the boilers?"

The man shook his head. "No, the boilers were not near where the explosion occurred."

"Maybe it was the Spanish," one of the men next to him claimed.

"Now why would they attack a grain ship?" Captain Morris grumbled.

"Men, please, let's not start making assumptions," Hanlon warned them. "Was there anything else that seemed out of the ordinary before the explosion?"

"Well … there was one thing," one of the men stated.

"What?" All eyes turned to him.

He swallowed hard and looked down. "I remember seeing a small crate sitting right up against one of the coal bunkers."

"And you're just telling us this now?" Captain Morris rounded on him.

The man jumped back. "Well, I didn't think anything of it! I thought maybe one of us just left it there and was going to come back for it!"

"Was it a piece of cargo perhaps?" Hanlon asked

"No. All the cargo is kept in a separate compartment from the coal bunkers," the captain stated.

Hanlon made some notes and finished taking statements from the crew before he came up to Harry and Edward. "So what did you gentlemen see?"

"Well, first we heard a loud bang," Edward explained. "Then we saw the ship on fire. Both of us went out to retrieve the men when we saw how bad it was."

"There was a large hole in the hull of the ship," Harry continued. "She started to go under."

"Was there anything you saw that seemed suspicious?" Hanlon questioned.

"Not that I can think of," Edward answered.

"I've been around ships almost all my life," Harry said. "This wasn't the result of some average coal fire."

"Well, from what the engineer told me, it doesn't appear to be a boiler explosion," Hanlon said. "Hell, it could've been a bomb for all we know."

The comment caught both keepers off guard.

"Are you suggesting this is sabotage?" Edward asked.

"I don't think we should rule anything out," Hanlon stated. "I'm interested to know which company this ship is insured with."

"You think this may be connected to the other ships?" Harry asked.

"Like I said, anything is possible." Hanlon shrugged. "At least it doesn't seem as bad as it could have been." His nonchalance surprised Edward.

"People died." Edward stated the obvious.

"Yes, and that's terrible, but with an explosion like this, it could've been much worse," Hanlon explained.

While Edward could see his point, he also found his lack of concern to be poor form. And his suggestions about sabotage left him feeling uneasy, as the thought had already crossed his mind too. A horn sounded in the distance and they went to look out the window. The RC *Gresham* had arrived and pulled up next to the *Cornelius Wade*. It got to work using its own hoses to put out the fire. Sometime later the crew had managed to extinguish the flames, which had left behind a mangled mess. The heat from the fire and the force of the explosion had caused the iron to twist and splinter. The wood had all burned away and a metal skeleton was all that was left. After that was done, the *Gresham*'s crew investigated whether anyone was left on board and was able to pump water out of the ship's hull to keep it afloat. A few hours later, the *Wade* was towed to port by the *Gresham*. There would be an investigation into the cause of the explosion.

The remaining members of the *Wade*'s crew were welcomed to stay the night at the keeper's quarters until they could find other lodging or make their way back home. The captain and a few others opted to go with their damaged ship back to port, using the lifeboat to meet the *Gresham*. Edward went back to the lighthouse and resumed his watch. He and Harry took turns checking on the men and the lighthouse throughout the night.

༒

After the excitement had worn down, Marie and Anna went back to bed. Anna looked over to see Marie facing away from her. Her sister was still angry at her from the previous night. Anna in turn was none too happy with her sister after the scolding she had gotten from their mother and the extra set of chores she was given. The tension had made helping the shipwrecked men tonight awkward as well. Both girls only spoke briefly to each other when they needed to.

"Anna." She heard a soft voice call her name and she turned over to face the little boy who had been in the cave.

Her eyes grew wide. "You shouldn't be here," she whispered harshly. "If Marie sees you she'll tell Mama again."

"Don't worry about her," the boy told her. "She's asleep."

"Why did you take her doll?" she asked. "She blamed me for it and I got in trouble."

"I thought it would be a nice surprise for her," he explained. "So she could have one of her favorite things in our hideaway."

"Well, don't do it again," Anna commanded. "Now go, I have to get to sleep."

"I think I should get my sister to get her to come to the cave," he said.

"Marie will never go there again, don't bother."

"My sister will convince her," he said. "She needs to see our secret." With that the boy turned and glided out of the room.

CHAPTER 7- CELEBRATION

The girls were eating their breakfast a few days later when Edward came down to see them. After giving it some thought, he had decided to take them to see the vaudeville show. He felt that the family deserved a reward for their hard work with the ship explosion. Frances had also insisted, her way of wanting to celebrate her husband's heroics. Edward had also recently learned of the fight the girls had had and he was hoping that being able to go out for some entertainment would ease the tension.

"How are you girls doing this morning?" he asked cheerfully.

"Very well, Father," Marie answered.

"I've been better," Anna grumbled.

"I would like to thank you two for helping the men the other night," he said. "I know that was quite a task for you and you both acted very maturely."

"At least someone knows it," Anna said, to which Marie shot her daggers.

"You two are going to have to forgive each other

eventually," Edward mused.

"Only if she apologizes," Marie stated, looking down at her food.

"As should you," Anna exclaimed. "For all of those extra chores I got!"

"You would not have gotten all those chores if you hadn't stolen my doll!"

"I didn't!" Anna yelled. "I don't know how many times I have to tell you that!"

"And how many times do I have to tell you that it is not possible for her to have ended up there herself!" Marie yelled back.

"Girls, enough!" Edward was tired of their bickering. "Marie, did you get your doll back undamaged?"

"Yes," she murmured.

"And Anna, do you understand taking things that aren't yours is wrong?" he asked.

"Yes, but I didn't take it!" Anna shot back.

"Alright, regardless of who did what, there is a simple way to solve this," Edward explained. "You will apologize to each other at the same time. Now, on the count of three. One, two, three…"

"I'm sorry," both girls said grudgingly.

"Good, see how easy that was?" he said. "Now I have good news for you both." He pulled the tickets to the show out of his pocket. He'd gotten them yesterday after getting assurances from the theater manager that the show was suitable for young children.

Marie looked at the tickets, then up at her father. "Really? We're going?" Her excitement was hard to contain.

"Yes, my dears." He smiled at the two.

"Thank you!" Both girls jumped up and hugged their father.

"Now finish your breakfast," he said. "I'm going to bed now."

"Oh, don't forget, the fireworks are tonight!" Anna cried after him.

"Ah, I almost forgot." Edward smiled. "Happy Independence Day."

Edward went upstairs with a bounce in his step now that he was reminded of the firework display tonight. And he was also excited about the vaudeville show. It would be a nice escape from his day-to-day work.

Just as he was about to go to bed, there was a knock at the front door. Edward groaned and made himself decent before heading back downstairs to find David Wilkins on the porch. He brought news that the preliminary investigation into the ship's explosion was complete. Edward ushered him into the office so he and Harry could discuss it with him.

"Based on the evidence found on the ship, it was determined that the explosion was caused by some minor explosives and, judging by the residue found, likely placed right inside one of the coal bunkers. They went off either when they were heated up enough by the coal or when there was a coal fire. One of the men also mentioned a mysterious crate," Wilkins explained. "We haven't found any evidence of that crate in the ruins, but if there were explosives in it, there should have been nothing of the sort on board. The only cargo that was supposed to be on that ship was grain and potatoes. Needless to say, this appears to be an act of sabotage."

"So any idea who did it?" Edward asked.

"That's what we are trying to figure out," Wilkins replied. "The captain vouched for each of his men's integrity, saying he trusted all of them. The first mate did mention he saw a strange man near where the ship was docked hours before she set off. At the time he thought maybe he worked on another ship, but now he realizes he should have taken more notice. The captain and crew members also swear they had no knowledge of how that crate got on the ship. They only packed the grain and potatoes, but someone must have stowed it in there secretly."

"You don't think it was the Spanish, do you?" Harry asked.

"That would be highly unlikely," Wilkins explained. "The explosives appeared to be made from regular household items so it could have been the work of any civilian. And the ship itself was of no military or national consequence, so there would be no motive for attacking it."

"Then is there any indication that this ship is connected to the others that were wrecked recently?" Harry asked.

"There doesn't appear to be," Wilkins replied. "This ship was insured with another company, not with East Knox."

"Maybe it was a personal vendetta then," Edward suggested.

"The investigation is ongoing." He shrugged. "Oh, and sadly, one of the men died from his injuries at the hospital. Another is still clinging to life."

"Sorry to hear that," Harry said.

"It is unfortunate," Wilkins agreed. "On a lighter note, I heard the crew gave you two so much praise for your rescue that now you're both being considered for lifesaving medals."

Edward's cheeks turned red. "What?"

Harry grumbled, "Don't see why, just doing our job."

"Still, it takes brave men to put their own lives in danger to save others. Don't know if I could do it." Wilkins stood. "Well, I must be going, gentlemen. Good day to you both."

They bid the man farewell and proceeded to take their rest. For his part, Edward didn't particularly like being the center of attention so the idea of being awarded a medal filled him with embarrassment. And he agreed with Harry. He didn't think of their deeds as anything heroic, just what any good person would do if they had the means. He didn't take this job for the glory of it, only because he liked to help people.

When the sun went down, it proved to be a warm Fourth of July night. Frances and Margaret took the children out to sit at the edge of the cliff overlooking the beach. From that vantage point they could see the fireworks being set off from the boardwalk pier. A loud boom sounded and the sky was filled with thousands of glistening sparks. Edward watched from the lighthouse balcony and looked down at his family below. He was filled with a sense of nostalgia, for the day always held a special place in his heart. He first met Frances on the Fourth of July thirteen years ago. It was a better time then. They were both young and in love and so, so happy. But now there was a dissonance in their marriage. They still loved each other, but they weren't happy and they constantly got under the other's skin. He hoped one day, hopefully by next Fourth of July, their own spark would be back.

༄

Lily knocked on the door of the hotel room that Hanlon had rented for the night. The hotel was located a few towns over and it was expensive to rent one of the rooms, but Hanlon was willing to pay the price at the fancy establishment. Lily and her husband were staying there for a social event and Lily used the excuse of "feeling poorly" to stay in her hotel room while her husband was preoccupied.

Hanlon opened the door and a cheerful smile lit up his face. "Lily, my dear!" He closed the door after her and swept her into his arms before kissing her fiercely.

"My, you're in a swell mood," she laughed as he let her go.

"I always am whenever I see you," he cooed. "I got you something too."

"Oh really?" She raised an eyebrow. "Is it going to spark questions?"

"Not if you keep it well hidden," he remarked with a mischievous glint in his eyes.

From his pocket, he pulled out a small trinket box that was half the size of his palm. It was silver with flower engravings on it. Lily took it and examined it, turning it over in her palm and opening it to see the black velvet–lined interior. "Oh, it's so pretty," she marveled. "It must have cost a pretty penny though."

"Nothing's too expensive for you," he reminded her. "And besides, I had a great day at work and wanted to celebrate."

"For what?" she asked.

"I finished a case today," he replied.

"Which one? I've been out of town," she

explained. "Haven't caught up on all of my news."

"Remember those men who pretended to get work at Crawford's restaurant back in town and then robbed it clean?" he asked.

"Oh yes. You found them?"

"Sure did." He nodded. "Found where they were hiding out. We guarded the doors to the house and ordered them to come out. When they finally did, we made a grab for them."

"Did they put up a fight?" she inquired with excited eyes.

"Did they ever!" he exclaimed. "Came out with guns ready and tried shooting at us. I jumped on one of them and got him to the ground. I was able to subdue him while the other officers grabbed his partner."

"How terrifying, but so exciting!" She beamed. "You're so brave." Of course what she didn't know was that he was exaggerating some of the details. The police had hidden out and caught the robbers by surprise when they were trying to leave the house. They had put up a fight, but they had no guns, only their fists.

"Oh no." He shook his head with false modesty. "It was all in a day's work."

"You're too modest," she said as she kissed his cheek. "I'm so proud of you."

"Thanks, love." He smiled at her.

She looked contemplative for a second. "Oh, and what about that other case? The one with the shipwrecks? I heard about that ship explosion off Wawenock Point."

He hung his head. "No new leads sadly. This latest shipwreck doesn't appear to have anything to do with the other ones, strange as it was."

"Well, I know you, if no one else is able to do it, you'll find the men behind it and bring them to justice," she reassured him.

"Oh, believe me," he said seriously, "when I find those idiots, I'll kill them."

☙

Edward was sitting in the watch room when the singing began again. So she had returned. He had not heard from or seen the mysterious woman on the beach for the past few nights. He figured all the commotion with the ship explosion had kept her away. He knew it was better to stay where he was, but he had to see her, if only to stop his suspicions. As much as he disbelieved in her being an ancient creature, he couldn't push the thought from the back of his mind.

He walked out of the lighthouse and was met with a cool breeze coming in from the sea. The light from the moon created eerie shadows of the lighthouse and keeper's quarters on the ground. The sky was clear and stars were shining. Edward couldn't help but feel an odd sense of peace, almost ominous in that it could end at any moment. As he walked toward the shore he could hear the breaking of waves more clearly. They were in a battle with the woman's voice, seeing who could be louder. He didn't need to say anything when he finally approached her, for she turned immediately. Her violet eyes were shining with mischief.

"So you came back to me," she mused. "I missed you the last few nights."

"I've been preoccupied," he said. "But I do need to figure out who you are."

"Couldn't resist, could you?" She smiled her wicked smile at him again. "And yes, I saw the explosion. Made a hero out of you, I see."

Edward felt the heat come to his face. "Are you mocking the saving of lives?"

"On the contrary, I find it quite commendable," she replied. "Especially considering I do the opposite."

"Are you telling me that you kill people?" he asked with disdain.

"Only when I'm hungry." She shrugged

"Hungry?" he asked in confusion and horror.

"A girl needs to eat," she stated matter-of-factly. "And I have quite a big appetite. So tell me, did you find out my little secret?"

He tried to ignore her previous comment, not wanting to comprehend what "eating" would mean for her, and instead answered her question. "Let me take a wild guess," he sneered. "A siren."

"Good man, you've done your research." She began to circle around him again, almost as if inspecting him.

"Do you really expect me to believe that you're some ancient creature out of mythology?" He cocked an eyebrow at her.

She gave him a cold glare. "Believe it or not, it's the truth."

"Do you think I'm a fool?" he spat. "The only truth here is that you're either crazy or you're a murderer; maybe both. I'm afraid you can't be here any longer and I'll have to turn you over to the proper authorities."

He went to grab her arm so that he could detain her, but she swiftly moved outside of his grasp. Instead, she quickly grabbed the back of his head, pulling him near her face. She placed her other hand roughly on his throat and thrust his head back. He wasn't able to free himself from her grip.

"I am sorry that I am inclined to believe that men who do not listen to truth are indeed fools," she whispered harshly in his ear. "I can be dangerous, Edward, I can tear you apart, so show some courtesy." Then she shoved him away from her and he stumbled backward.

"Don't ever touch me!" he cried, rubbing at his throat. "How are you that strong?" How was she capable of this and how did she know his name?

"What part of ancient magical creature do you not understand?" she asked, annoyed. "Perhaps you require more proof?" She stretched an arm out toward the ocean and in a sweeping motion brought it forward again. A large wave rose up and slammed against the beach in that instant, soaking Edward's pants from the knees down.

He stumbled back, mouth agape. "This…this just isn't possible," he mumbled.

"Oh, but it is, my dear," she said silkily. "Come to me." She started humming again and Edward's body once again moved to her of its own accord.

"Stop it; let me go," he grunted, trying to fight against the force.

"Why should I?" She walked toward him. "You are quite the challenge, honorable man that you are, and I enjoy challenges."

"Challenge?" He was dumbfounded. "What do you want with me?"

"Do you know why I draw men in with my song?" she asked. He just shook his head. "I feed off them, off their energy. But I can only do it when they have lost all their senses at my will and are in complete delusional ecstasy."

"That's why you tried seducing me," he said. "So you could sleep with me and then feed off me."

"Do you really think I need to sleep with men to feed off them?" she scoffed. "My song is enough. Although, I suppose I wouldn't mind doing so with you. But as I said, you are too honorable of a man. You would never be unfaithful to your wife, despite whatever ... affliction she may have."

"Do not speak of my wife in such a manner," he hissed.

"If it pleases you, I won't, but regardless, I'll get you eventually," she said, her tone growing more serious.

"No you won't, because I will never give into you." He became defiant.

"What's the matter, Edward?" she asked. "Afraid you might experience some pleasure?" She ghosted a hand down his torso.

"Stop it." He stepped back. "You might as well just leave these shores and find yourself better prey."

"I'm not going anywhere," she said in a sharp tone. "I've been here longer than you, longer than this structure even." She tilted her head toward the lighthouse. "So I'm not leaving, but you may be."

"Do not threaten me." His voice was deadly.

"I'm not threatening you, I'm warning you," she replied, a malicious smirk gracing her beautiful, but frightening face. "There are many souls that haunt these shores, some who have died at my hand, I'll admit, but many more who have not. Some spirits are out for blood, and I'm not even the worst of them." With that she turned and walked away from him. "I think it's best if you go now." She waved her hand at him.

This time he had no problem helping the force that was driving him to go. He clambered his way up the rocky cliff and rushed back to the lighthouse. He quickly locked the door behind him and looked out the window. Once again, she was gone. *What the hell is going on?* he thought. Was he going mad and hallucinating? But he could still feel where she had squeezed his throat and his pants were still wet. She was real, that much was for sure. Was it possible that magic was real after all? Was this woman really what she claimed to be? He never thought such things were possible, but after tonight, he would have to reevaluate his beliefs.

CHAPTER 8- THE VAUDEVILLIANS

Saturday had finally come and the girls were in their rooms getting ready to see the vaudeville show. Edward had tried to put the encounter with the siren out of his mind, but it wasn't easy. Every time he made his way to and from the quarters or the lighthouse, he would make sure she was nowhere in sight. He had no idea to what extent the siren was capable, but he didn't want to find out and he had no idea how to make her go away, if he even could. Tonight, though, he decided not to think about it and just wanted to enjoy some good old-fashioned entertainment. He had even slept more that day so that he would be refreshed for his nightly shift. Harry had agreed to take the first shift so that Edward could take his family out. Margaret had kindly offered to stay in that night to take care of Thomas so Edward wouldn't have to leave him with family members in town. Prior to leaving the house, Edward trimmed his mustache and combed his hair neatly to the side. He dressed in one of his better suits and stood back to admire his appearance in the mirror. For once, he thought he actually looked like a typical late Victorian gentleman. Then Frances walked into the bedroom and he noticed that she had not changed.

"You're not dressed yet?" he asked. "We have to go soon."

"I'm not going," she said quietly.

He stopped. "What do you mean you're not going?"

"I have to stay here, I can't leave." She took to sitting at the window again.

"No you don't," he said, walking over to her. "If you're worried about Thomas, Margaret is going to take care of him."

"It doesn't matter; I can't leave," she whispered.

"You're the one who insisted we go." The annoyance in his voice was obvious. "The girls want you to come. They will be disappointed if you don't go. And the show will be fun."

"I know." Her voice became shakier and she seemed on the verge of tears. "But I can't go, I just can't."

"This has to stop." He grabbed her arm and tried to pull her up. "Get dressed, you're going."

"No!" she cried and yanked her arm away. "Don't touch me! I'm not going!"

"Oh, so now I can't even touch you!" he exclaimed. "My own wife I can't touch. I don't know what you want from me anymore! Every time I reach out to you, try to talk to you, try to help you, you recede further into yourself."

"I can't help it!" She was crying. "It's not like I want this."

"Well then I'll have to take you back to Dr.

Neumann," he said. "Obviously, the treatment he prescribed isn't helping."

"Because there is nothing that can help."

"That's because you are not even trying!" he yelled. "From the start you were wary of the treatment you were prescribed. You never even wanted it to work. I know he said to get more rest, but you sleep so much you'd think he had told you to go into hibernation. Margaret's running herself ragged doing what you're supposed to be doing and it's not like I can always be there to help when I have to work. And our poor children… you act like Thomas isn't even yours."

"Stop!" she cried in exasperation. "Stop yelling at me! I know I'm a horrible person! Do you know what it's like to give birth to a child and then feel nothing for it?"

He stopped. "So you admit it?" He swallowed hard, trying to control his anger.

"You're the one who wanted me to have him," she growled. "You're the one who pushed me into it." Then she paused, before adding sharply, "This is *your* fault."

His nostrils flared as he breathed heavily. "How dare you say that to me?" God, he wanted to slap her so badly for saying that. "Do you think I wanted this for you? For our family?" He turned from her then and hurriedly shrugged his suit jacket on. "Fine, stay here tonight. Go cry yourself to sleep and wallow in your misery. But I'm going to have a good time tonight with *my* daughters."

He turned and left the room. He could hear her crying and instantly regretted his words, knowing they would come to no good. He walked down the stairs and called for the girls.

Marie and Anna had been listening in their room the entire time.

"Don't say anything," Marie warned Anna.

The younger girl nodded and the two went to join their father downstairs, acting like nothing had happened.

☙

The family had arrived on the boardwalk half an hour before the show started, getting there quicker than expected. The girls were sad their mother had not come and they could feel the tension coming off their father, but they tried to remain cheerful regardless. The family walked up to the bustling theater and handed their tickets to the doorman.

The lobby of the theater was filled with people all dressed in their best and conversing with each other. The three made their way into the dimly lit theater. The floors were covered with red carpeting, the same color that graced the velvet curtains on the stage and the seat cushions. Gilded arches framed the stage and an orchestra was set up in front. The family found a group of seats about midway between the doors and the stage. Anna looked up at the balconies, hearing voices coming from above.

Edward, meanwhile, was looking at the playbill when he heard a voice call to him. "Hey, Ed, is that you?"

He looked up to see a round, bald man with a gray mustache. "Walt, my good man, I feel like I haven't seen you in years," Edward greeted the man cheerily, as he got up and shook his hand.

The girls looked over to the man. "That's the carousel operator," Anna whispered to Marie, who just nodded.

"Took your girls out to see the show, I see," Walter said to Edward. "Where's your wife?"

"She wasn't feeling well," Edward lied. He had become used to making up excuses for her.

"Oh, well tell Fran I give her my best," he said. "I have to help finish setting up for the acts."

"You work here too!" Anna exclaimed, only to be nudged by her sister for her outburst.

"Well, I hope you girls didn't think I could make a living off operating a carousel alone," he laughed then tilted his hat toward them. "Good night to you ladies, I hope you enjoy the show. Same to you, Ed."

"Thanks, goodnight, Walt." Edward saw the man off then sat down again.

"How does he know you, Father?" Marie asked. "He knew we were your daughters last time we went on the carousel, but I do not recall ever seeing him before then."

"Walter's an old family friend," Edward explained. "You met him once when we first moved to Wawenock Point, but he was a lot thinner and his hair was on his head, not his face."

Marie laughed, before Anna silenced her. "Shhh!" she whispered. "The show's starting."

The orchestra started to play a number, signaling to patrons to get to their seats. The lights dimmed on the audience and grew brighter on the stage. As the latecomers took their seats, the theater became quiet. The stage curtains separated and a spotlight shined on the center of the stage. A man with smoothly combed back black hair and a thick mustache stood in the center of the stage. He had on a dark gray tailored suit and a bright red bow tie.

"Ladies and gentlemen," he announced, his voice rebounding around the theater, "I would like to welcome you all to our grand Saturday Night Spectacular!" The audience clapped and then the man continued, "Before the show begins, I would like to ask a few favors of you all on behalf of management. Gentlemen, please refrain from smoking inside the theater and ladies, please remove your hats so those behind you may see the show. Please do not talk during the acts and if you wish to show your approval of a performance, you need only do so by using the following motion with your hands." In comedic style he began to clap slowly, which earned a few laughs. "Now enough with the lecturing and onto the show! Tonight you will see acts that will amaze you, even some that will confound you! You will never see anything like it again in your life! Without further ado, please give a warm round of applause for our first act: The Atlantic Acrobats!"

Applause filled the room as the man stepped off into the wings and the second set of curtains opened. The stage was occupied by five men in tight gym clothes. They did handstands and flips of all kinds and took turns doing circling elements on a bar. A few excited gasps filled the theater as they used poles to hold themselves up in the air at right angles. They then formed a pyramid shape by standing on each other's shoulders. Loud applause broke out in the room as the men broke formation and bowed before leaving the stage.

Next up was a dog act with a Jack Russell terrier that pushed a ball with his paws. A larger Border collie jumped through hoops. The next act was the short play *The Washerwoman*, which showcased two immigrant women with over-the-top accents, arguing about the proper way to wash their husbands' clothes. One was Irish who insisted that they were best washed with a little bit of whiskey and the other was Italian who said it was best to not wash them at all as it had worked for her for years. They continued arguing until in the end, the Irish woman passed out drunk from the whiskey and the Italian woman, now angry, slipped on the floor trying to smack the Irish woman awake. The crowd loved it, letting out a raucous chorus of laughter and relishing in the exploitation of the stereotypes.

Next up was the pair of tap dancers who had displayed their talents the day Marie and Anna had come to the boardwalk. Their act started slowly at first, with each one trying to outdo the other's movements. By the end of the act they were tapping faster and in sync much to the audience's satisfaction. They were followed by a quartet who played their own rendition of one of Beethoven's orchestral numbers and added their own comical lyrics to it. There was a brief intermission during which Edward went to go get some snacks while door prizes were given out to audience members.

Once the intermission ended and everyone was back in their seats, the curtains opened to reveal two men on stage with a group of musicians behind them. One of them was black; the other was only painted that way. The black man sang in a deep baritone voice while dancing and the black-faced man frantically moved around the stage, jumping and dancing and cutting into the song every so often with a jibe. To the crowd, there was nothing unusual about this routine and they applauded it as they had the others.

This was followed by a slapstick comedy routine. The eighth act was Jack Porter with his ventriloquist dummy. He sat on a chair in the middle of the stage with the doll on his lap. The doll's wood face had bright red cheeks and large eyes and he was dressed as a newspaper boy.

"So, Bobby Boy, got a good crowd tonight," Jack spoke.

"Ha, I've been given a better reception in a cemetery," the doll shot back and a few laughs could be heard from the crowd.

"Now that's not nice," Jack scolded. "These fine people came just to see you."

"Probably because you told them you'd be using me as firewood later." Bobby's higher-pitched voice went out across the crowd to more laughter.

"You know my mother's here tonight," Jack said pointing in the crowd.

"Oh, that's your mother." The dummy's voice was softer as he stared out into the audience. Then he added louder, "I thought someone let a horse into the building." The crowd burst into laughter and someone cackled loudly in the back.

"Hey, would you stop that!" Jack said, pushing the dummy's shoulder. "What's gotten into you tonight?"

"Well, I got some bad news today," Bobby answered sadly.

"Oh really, what's that?" Jack asked in concern.

"I read all us newspaper boys are going to be out of jobs." Bobby hung his head.

"Oh no, why's that?"

"Newspaper girls are cheaper."

"That's a darn shame. You can always get another job, though," Jack reassured him.

"I was already offered one."

"As what?"

"A table leg."

"A table leg? And what did you say to that?"

"I said are you kidding? I can't even stand on my own legs." The dummy's legs fell to either side of Porter's knee. "Oh no, not again."

"You know, I think you should see a doctor about that."

"See a doctor? I think you better have your head examined." Bobby shook his head disapprovingly. "I'm a hunk of wood; I'm better off going to a carpenter."

Jack raised an eyebrow at him. "You know, maybe we'll have that bonfire after all."

"Listen, wise guy, don't make me tell the manager what you've got in that trunk of yours," Bobby snapped.

"I don't know what you're talking about."

"Oh, those weren't bottles I heard clanking around in there?"

"Are you insinuating that I'm a drunk?" Jack's voice rose in mock anger.

"No, I'm just saying you're well-watered!" More laughter from the crowd.

"Why you…" Jack's voice began, before it was immediately cut off by Bobby's.

"Say, look at that gal over there!" The dummy's head turned toward the left side of the audience.

"Oh, don't you start that again!" Jack's voice rose again.

"Hey, I don't start anything!" Bobby defended himself. "But I sure do finish everything!" One of the doll's wooden eyes winked at the crowd as more laughter arose.

"Say goodnight, everyone," Jack called out. "Bobby's gotta get some shut-eye!" The crowd applauded as the man carried his dummy off the stage.

The curtains closed again for a few more moments before the announcer came out again. "Now, folks, the man you've all been waiting for." His excited voice boomed across the theater. "I am pleased to present to you all Marco the Magnificent!"

The crowd applauded as the curtains opened. A man in a top hat and coattails stood on the stage. He had tanned skin and dark hair and eyes. A beautiful woman stood to his right in a bright blue dress. A large rectangular box with a velvet curtain stood behind them. A table was off to the left.

"Thank you, ladies and gentlemen, for that marvelous reception." The man's deep voice came clear across the audience. He took off his hat and held it out before the audience. "Observe here, that there is nothing inside of this hat." He then smacked the hat so that the crown crumpled to the brim. He reached into it, stretching the hat back out, and pulled out a bouquet of flowers. Some "oohs" and cheers came from the audience.

He placed his top hat back on and threw the flowers into the audience. An overly excited woman nearly fell onto the people in front of her to catch it. "Now I will ask my assistant to please lie down on this table," he said as he walked over to it. The woman followed him and he held out his hand, helping her to lie down. He walked around the back side of the table and waved his hands over it. He leaned over one side of the table and removed the legs from it, then did the same on the other side. The table seemed to be floating in midair. The crowd burst into applause. Marco then replaced the legs of the table and helped his assistant off of it.

"Now, I will need a volunteer from the audience," he announced. The assistant held up a bag for him and he pulled out a white card. "Whoever is in seat F21, please come to the stage."

The audience members turned at once to see what seat they were in. Anna gasped before yelling out, "That's me!" Her father turned to her in surprise. Marie gave her an angry look, jealous that her sister was lucky enough to be picked over her.

"Well, come on up, dear, don't be shy!" Marco called out and waved for the girl to make her way to the stage. Anna hurriedly got up and tried not to trip over anyone as she raced up the stairs to the stage.

"What's your name, little girl?" he asked once Anna had made her way to the stage.

"Anna," she replied eagerly.

"Well, Anna, if you'd be so kind as to follow my assistant," he instructed as he turned to the crowd. "Before your very eyes, ladies and gentlemen, I am going to make young Anna here disappear once she steps inside that box."

The assistant walked over and picked up a piece of cloth from a chair. "But first, I am going to need Anna to put on this magical cloak, for it will allow her to help me complete the trick." The assistant held up the velvet red cloak embroidered with gold thread. Anna put it on and it made her feel like a queen.

"Very good, my dear! Now if you will please." Marco gestured to the box and the assistant helped Anna into it. As she stepped inside, the assistant whispered to her, "No matter what happens, don't scream, alright?"

Anna was confused but nodded anyway. Marco stepped up to the box as the assistant closed the curtains hanging over the opening. It was dark inside and Anna started to feel afraid. "Now on the count of three, I will open the curtains again," she heard the magician's voice say from outside the box.

Suddenly, she felt herself falling from the stage. She let out a "whoa!" as she fell, ignoring the assistant's warning. However, it was doubtful that anyone could hear her from beyond the stage. Anna found herself in a dimly lit room as she landed on a pile of mattresses.

"Scary falling through there, isn't it?" a voice from behind her came. She turned to see an elderly man.

"I'll say. What happened?" she asked him.

"Trap door," he responded, pointing upward. "It's part of the trick. Come on, I'll lead you upstairs."

Back on stage, Marco was counting, "One...two...three..." The assistant opened the curtains to reveal that Anna had indeed disappeared. Several audience members gasped. "Now if you will turn behind you..."

"I'm here!" a little girl's voice called out from one of the top balconies where no one was sitting. A girl with blonde curls and a matching red cloak appeared at the railing of the balcony. The little girl's face was too far away to be recognizable to any of the audience members—all but two, that is. Edward felt his heart race as he realized the little blonde girl in the balcony was not his child. "That's not your sister," Edward whispered to Marie, who too had realized this.

Regardless, the crowd burst into applause as Marco and his assistant took a bow. Edward turned when he felt a tap on his shoulder. "You can go get her backstage after the show," one of the theater ushers whispered to him.

The last act of the night was a man juggling while playing a harmonica attached to his head with a metal device. At this point, some of the audience members were starting to get up and leave. After the final act ended, all of the performers came out to take one last bow as the audience clapped. The announcer declared that the show was over and soon the remaining audience members filed out of the theater. Edward and Marie followed one of the ushers backstage where they passed several dressing rooms. They got to what looked like a dining area where many of the performers were eating refreshments. The black man sat at a side table where another performer was talking to him. While he appeared jovial onstage, now he looked sullen and exhausted. And it didn't go unnoticed that many of the other performers kept their distance from him. Finally, they saw Anna sitting with Jack Porter, who was showing her his dummy.

"Well, I was worried I'd never see you again," Edward said as he went to her.

Anna turned to him. "Papa, look, it's Bobby Boy!"

"I see," Edward said.

"Jack Porter." The ventriloquist offered his hand to Edward.

"Edward Ashman," Edward said, taking his hand.

"Your daughter is just wonderful company."

"Better than this guy anyway," the dummy chimed in.

"I'm sure she is," Edward laughed, turning to his daughter. "You had quite the interesting night."

"Yes, but it was scary," Anna said. "I fell through a trap door!"

"That always gets them."

Edward turned to see Walter.

"I'm assuming you're responsible for this?" Edward asked, a small smile tugging at his lips.

"It's why I go around the audience," he responded. "Try to see if anyone in the audience looks like our little girl so we can do the disappearing act. And I happened to notice your Anna did."

"And who was the other little girl?" Edward inquired.

"Our daughter," the sweet voice of a woman said. Edward turned to see the magician's assistant walk up to the group with her daughter beside her and Marco behind her. She smiled at him and his heart stopped. *The siren!* He blinked and looked at the woman again. Her features changed to that of an ordinary woman. His mind was playing tricks on him. *It had to be her smile, it looked just like hers.*

"So you two are married?" Anna's abrupt question interrupted his thoughts.

"Yes, but don't go telling anyone, it might ruin my reputation," Marco answered humorously as his wife nudged him in the side.

Marie studied their daughter before turning to her sister and commenting, "You two could be twins."

"What's your name?" Anna asked.

"Clara," the girl answered quietly and moved closer to her mother.

"She's shy," her mother said while she stroked her hair.

"So what do you do if no one in the audience looks like her?" Marie questioned.

"I do another trick," Marco explained. "Although I must admit, it's not nearly as exciting as the disappearing act."

"This isn't fair though," Anna grunted. "Now I know how the trick works and it isn't magic at all!"

Edward mused to himself, *If you want real magic I'll introduce you to the siren.*

"Well, I have plenty of other tricks that require real magic," Marco said as he placed his hand behind her ear and pulled out a gold coin and handed it to her.

"How'd you do that one?" Anna asked.

He shook a finger at her and winked. "A magician never reveals his secrets."

"I wish you'd do us all a favor and reveal them already so that a better act can have your spot." The Italian woman from the short came over to grab some food. This time her accent was gone.

"Darling, you'll never have the ninth spot, with or without me," Marco scoffed.

The woman shot daggers at him, but Edward interrupted before more words could be exchanged. "So you aren't Italian then?" he asked.

"God no," she replied. "I'm Jewish."

"Like that's any better."

Edward turned to see the Irish woman come over, her accent still very much intact.

"But you are Irish, I see," Edward commented.

"I am, but if the Irish are going to be made fun of, I might as well make some money off it," she explained.

"Fair enough," Edward considered.

"I know an Irish woman," Anna chimed in. "Her name's Margaret Bancroft. Do you know her?"

The woman laughed. "You think all Irish people know each other?"

Anna's face turned red. Edward took that as the signal to leave. "Well, it was nice meeting you all," he said. "But I'm afraid we must be getting back." He would soon have to start his shift at the light.

Anna was reluctant to leave, but got up. "Goodbye, everyone!" she called, waving. They in turn waved and said goodbye as the family left.

"You said he's the lightkeeper right?" Jack asked Walter.

"Yes," the large man replied.

"I heard about that ship that exploded over there," Marco's wife added.

"Oh yes, it was a terrible accident," Walter acknowledged. "But it's not surprising. There are always problems when you're working around the shores... always."

∽

After Edward returned from the show, he relieved Harry of duty and took his place in the watch room. He was reading the newspaper when he heard the faint singing again. He sighed and leaned his head against the wall. She wasn't giving up. Why was the siren so desperate to make him her prey? He had never seen her before now in the four years he had lived here. The siren's call was tempting, he reluctantly admitted. He thought back to what the siren had said: *Afraid you might experience some pleasure?* After his several fights with his wife and how she had continuously pushed him away, the thought crossed his mind to go to the siren, let her embrace him, and fall victim to that uncontrollable ecstasy. It would be nice to feel the touch of a woman again; to feel wanted, loved even.

But he pushed those shameful thoughts aside and tried his best to ignore her for the rest of his shift, refusing to leave the safety of the lighthouse. When morning came he cleaned the lantern and lens and then grabbed one of Margaret's freshly made blueberry muffins to serve as his breakfast. He trudged upstairs and was relieved to see that Frances wasn't there. He fell asleep very easily. In his dream, he did what he had only ever imagined doing in his darkest moments. He crawled down the rocks, to the beach, to her: the siren. He fell into her arms and took her. When he jolted awake, the evidence of his arousal was apparent. *Dammit, how can that woman be so threatening yet so tempting at the same time?* he thought. And he wondered if she was implanting those dreams in his mind somehow. Whatever she was doing to his head, it seemed to be working. Guiltily, he got up and relieved himself.

CHAPTER 9- A CURSE

The next day, Anna was still reeling from the show. She became obsessed with the magic act and decided to give some of the tricks a try. Right now she was outside with one of her stuffed animals, trying to pull a coin out of its ear after her father explained how to do it. Marie, meanwhile, was reading in the downstairs parlor. She too was still thinking of the show and believed she had never seen anything so wonderful in all her life. Just as she was turning the page in her book, she heard a tapping on the window. She jumped at the sound and looked up to see a young girl standing there.

"Come outside!" the girl yelled through the glass.

"No!" was Marie's first reaction. She was taken aback. "Who are you?"

"I'm a friend of your sister's. Come outside," the girl replied.

"I've never seen you before." Marie grew frightened. "How do you know my sister? Where did you come from?"

"My brother introduced me to her," the girl said. "We come from the edge of town. Please come outside so we can play!"

"I don't think I should," Marie answered. "You shouldn't be here."

"It's okay, your sister is here," the girl insisted. "Please come out!"

Marie hesitated, but then agreed to. She had never seen this girl before or her brother, nor had Anna ever mentioned them. She really did not feel she should trust them. And why would their parents let them come here unannounced? Marie cautiously walked out of the house to where the girl was. Anna's stuffed animal sat on the grass, but the younger girl was nowhere to be seen.

"Where's my sister?" Marie asked. "You said she was here."

"Oh, she just left with my brother," the girl said.

"What are you playing at?" Marie took a step back.

"Nothing!" the girl swore. "I should introduce myself, how rude of me. My name is Louise."

"Marie," the other girl replied carefully. "How did your brother meet my sister?"

"One time when you were out in town," Louise answered.

"I think I would have remembered him." Marie eyed the girl suspiciously.

"I guess you just didn't see him." Louise tried to change the subject. "Now how about we go play?"

"I don't think so." Marie began to move back toward the house, but the girl was quickly at her side and grabbing her wrist. Her hand was ice cold and Marie could see now just how pale she was. She also couldn't help but notice that the girl's dress was ripped near the hem and seemed to be a few years old.

"You need to come with me," the girl pleaded. "I'll show you my favorite hiding spot. Your sister is probably there now with my brother."

Marie pulled her wrist back. "I don't want to!"

"You must!" the girl insisted. "I need to show you something there!" Marie didn't move from her spot. "Please, it'll just be for a moment."

"Fine, but make it quick."

The girl made her way around the back of the keeper's quarters and over to the rocks. Marie kept her distance the whole time, constantly looking back over her shoulder. She watched as Louise climbed down the rocks. Marie then realized where she was headed.

"The cave!" Marie gasped. "I'm not going back in there! You helped my sister put all of those things in there, didn't you?"

"Perhaps," Louise said coyly. "But we can have so much fun in there, I swear!"

"How can you have fun in a dark, dank cave?" Marie asked.

"Lots of ways." Louise shrugged. "You'd be surprised. But you must come. I have to show you something important."

"I don't care what it is, I'm not going in there!" Those were Marie's final words as she turned and walked quickly toward the keeper's quarters.

Louise gritted her teeth. "This is going to be harder than I thought," she said to herself as she watched Marie walk away.

Meanwhile, Louise's brother was leading Anna

farther and farther into the cave.

"How far are we going, Jimmy?" Anna asked, becoming worried. "It's getting too dark, I can't see."

"Not much further, hold up your lantern more," the boy replied, walking further into the cave. He traveled around a bend and stopped at the broad side of the cave wall. Anna followed him and he took the lantern from her hands. He held it up to the wall and Anna could see what looked like a bunch of red painted marks. Upon closer inspection she could see that they were actually letters and symbols. She had no idea what language they were in though; it certainly wasn't English and it didn't look like the French her sister studied in school.

"What language is that?" she asked him.

"Don't know," he said, studying the letters. "Some say it's an old form of English, others believe the Indians wrote it, and still others say the Vikings wrote this over a thousand years ago."

"And who says that?" she asked.

"Just people around town who know about it," he responded. "But it doesn't matter what the language is though, everyone always gives the same translation."

"What's that?" Anna was intrigued.

"It speaks of a curse and a sacrifice that must be made to lift it," he explained, his voice becoming distant as he became more and more transfixed on the writing.

Anna's heart skipped a beat. "What curse?"

"This land is cursed," he stated. "That's why so many people have died here."

"You can't be serious?" Anna's voice started shaking.

"And in order to lift the curse, a sacrifice of light and life must be made," his voice continued to drone on.

"Stop it! You're scaring me!" Anna cried.

"I had to tell you though; you needed to know." He turned to her.

"I'm leaving now," she muttered and turned to go. Jimmy followed her out. Louise stood by the entrance of the cave, but Anna noticed her sister was not with her.

"Where's Marie?" she asked, concerned.

"She wouldn't come," Louise replied. "But don't worry; we'll get her to eventually."

Anna walked out of the cave and the children followed her. Together, they pushed the large rock that covered the entrance of the cave back into place. It was their way of keeping others from finding out about their little hiding place. Anna walked back to the keeper's quarters, but Louise and Jimmy went the opposite way. They said they needed to head back to town, but Anna never saw them leave.

☙

The night was dark and the sky was filled with stars as Edward sat in the watch room. A steamer ship passed by and it made him think of the ship explosion again. Something kept bothering him about it. Wilkins said it wasn't likely that it was connected to the ships that had been attacked for the insurance money, but Edward wasn't so sure. If the explosives had been placed deliberately in the ship, then what, aside from some crazy personal revenge scheme, would be gained from it besides insurance money?

Perhaps the criminals had moved on to ships insured by other companies, or maybe they just got the wrong ship.

His thoughts were interrupted when he heard the singing again. There was absolutely no way he would go down to see the siren again. He refused to fall for her enchanting songs anymore, no matter how they tempted him. He was angry with himself for being aroused by her, but still very much frightened of her. Needless to say, he was glad the lighthouse was separating the two of them. Tonight, though, her song was sadder and softer. It made him drowsy and he soon fell into a light sleep.

In his dream, he found himself walking down the spiral staircase of the lighthouse. He opened the door and saw that he was not at Wawenock Point, but instead at a lighthouse in the middle of the open ocean. He walked around the outside of the tower but did not see anything but the expansive sea. Then the waves started to pick up and became harsher. One began to rise high up over his head and he quickly ran back inside and closed the door just as the wave crashed into the side of the building.

"We have to leave!" he heard Anna's voice call.

He turned to see both of his daughters running up the staircase. He followed them to the watch room. From the windows he could see the waves rising higher. Then one crashed into the window and he jumped back.

"We have to leave through the roof," Marie said and both girls ran up the second set of steps to the lantern room.

He went after them and could see the waves rising higher still. They had reached the lantern room and the waves hit the windows. Edward could feel his heart pound and the girls screamed. The waves crashed so hard they broke one of the windows and water began flooding into the room. He soon realized that the ocean itself had reached to the top of the tower. He and the girls quickly went outside to the observation deck, where water hit their feet. The tower was being sucked into the ocean and soon the water was up to his head. He tried swimming away, but it was of no use—he was being pulled under by the waves. He gasped for air and could get none.

Edward woke with a start. His heart pounded and extreme terror filled him. He looked out the window of the watch room and found that the ocean was a safe distance from the light. Harry was now sitting quietly next to him, reading his newspaper. The older man looked up in confusion at him, but said nothing. Edward felt himself calming down and he wiped sweat from his brow, or at least he hoped that was all it was.

CHAPTER 10- A GIFT TO THE SEA

The inspector came in the middle of July. The household had spent the previous two days making sure the lighthouse, the keeper's quarters, the storage shed, and the grounds were cleaned and organized. The inspector was a tall, lanky man with close-cropped hair and eyeglasses. He had a clean-cut mustache and carried a record book with him. Edward met him at the door of the keeper's quarters and welcomed him inside.

"Mr. Ashman, good morning," he greeted as he shook Edward's hand. He then did the same to Harry. "Good morning, Mr. Bancroft."

"Good morning, Mr. Lewis," Edward greeted in return.

The inspection started in the office where everything was neat and orderly. Lewis took a look at the watch and expenditure books to make sure Edward and Harry were writing appropriate records. He nodded as he sifted through the pages and seemed pleased with it. He went through the lower level of the quarters, closely inspecting the chimneys to make sure the soot wasn't built up and the kitchen to make sure it was not only clean, but free of fire hazards. When he seemed satisfied, the inspector moved upstairs to inspect the bedrooms, even though they had nothing to do with the operation of the lighthouse. The first two bedrooms were orderly; only a little bit of dust came off on the man's fingertips. Then they reached the girls' bedroom. They were greeted by an oily smell upon stepping foot into the room. As he made his way around one of the beds, Lewis stopped at the space in between them.

"Well, that explains the smell." He pursed his lips and made a note in his book.

In the space between the beds, the lantern had fallen off the nightstand, leaving shards of glass and a pool of kerosene on the floor. Edward felt his face go red. He had no idea when the lantern had fallen over, but the girls knew the inspector was coming and to make sure the house was clean.

"I am very sorry, sir," he stated quickly. "I told my daughters to clean this room."

"Well, they evidently missed a spot," was his curt reply.

Harry and Edward looked at each other before following the inspector through the rest of the rooms. Finally, he made his way out of the quarters and into the storage shed, which was perfectly tidy. Then they made their way into the lighthouse. As they walked up the spiral staircase, Lewis pulled on the banister, which had no give. When they came to the second landing, they heard an echo throughout the tower that sounded like the voice of a female, causing them to all stop in their tracks. Edward felt a chill run down his spine, as the voice had the distinct tone of the siren.

Lewis looked outside one of the windows. The two Ashman girls were outside in the yard playing. "Strange," he muttered. "Your wives stayed in the house, correct?"

"Yes, they were both in the parlor when we left," Harry answered.

Lewis cocked an eyebrow. The outside door had been locked behind them so there should have been no one in the lighthouse. He brushed it off and continued on. Edward prayed the strange woman with the ancient lineage wouldn't make a surprise appearance when they got further up the tower. They reached the watch room and Lewis made sure everything was clean. Then he went up to the lantern room. Edward let go of the breath he was holding when he saw there was no one else up there. He and Harry pulled off the bag from the Fresnel lens and pulled back the curtains a little bit to allow some light in. Lewis took to inspecting the Fresnel lens, making sure the glass was clean and not cracked. Then he looked at the oil lamp within the lens and the lighthouse's clockwork mechanism to make sure they were in proper working order. He also went outside to make sure the railings on the decks of the tower were stable.

When Lewis was satisfied, they made their way outside. The two keepers waited while Lewis made some notes in his book. "Well, aside from the overturned lantern, everything else was up to standard. But as this is your first strike in one of these inspections, I wouldn't worry about it this time."

Edward breathed a sigh of relief at that and the two men bade goodbye to Lewis. When the man was out of sight, Edward called to his daughters. "Marie! Anna! Come here now!" When they both made their way to him, he asked, "So who dropped the lantern in your bedroom?"

The girls looked at him in confusion. "I didn't do it," Marie said.

"Me neither."

"Well, one of you must have," he stated. "The inspector was not happy."

"It was probably her," Marie said, pointing at her sister. "I made sure everything was neat and tidy before I left the house."

"Hey! I did my cleaning too today!" Anna yelled. "You could've knocked it over and didn't even realize it!"

"I'm not clumsy like you!" Marie yelled back.

"Enough!" Edward shouted at them. "Both of you go upstairs and clean it now."

"Yes, sir," they muttered in unison and made their way upstairs.

The girls went to their room and started to clean up the oil and glass. "I swear I didn't do it, Marie," Anna said sincerely.

"I didn't either," Marie swore. "Do you think maybe it was Mother or Peggy?"

"Could have been," Anna considered. "You don't think Daisy got into the house, do you?"

"No, I doubt it." Marie stood, taking the oil-soaked rags with her. "I'll go get another lantern from the storage shed."

Anna walked over to the window and saw Louise standing outside. The girl waved at her, a devious smile on her face, before she ran off in the other direction. And suddenly Anna understood.

Anna and Marie were outside on the front lawn taking care of the flowers they had planted. The sun was beating down and the petals were wilting. Daisy stalked around the side of the house, searching for any mice. Anna called the cat over and as she walked by Anna petted her back. The cat rolled over to allow Anna to rub her belly. While running her fingers through the coarse fur, Anna was deep in thought.

"It was Louise," Anna finally said. "She's the one who knocked over the lantern."

"What?" Marie asked incredulously. "How do you know? How did she get in the house?"

"I saw her outside in the yard after we cleaned it up. I don't know how she got in the house." Anna shrugged. "She must have slipped in when no one was looking."

"Why would she do it?"

"I think she was angry with you for not going into the cave," Anna explained timidly.

Marie fumed, "That brat! She has no business being here anyway, let alone in our house!"

Marie's thoughts were stopped short when she looked up toward the shore and saw their mother walking toward the water. Their mother had been acting strangely the past few days. She moved about in a daze and quite a few times they heard her muttering to herself. They didn't know if it was the fight with their father or something else that had happened to her the night they saw the vaudeville show, but something was definitely not the same about her after that.

Marie watched as Frances made her way down the

rocky slope to the beach.

"What's Mother doing?" Marie asked. Then she noticed she was carrying something in her arms. "What's she carrying?"

Anna looked up and craned her neck to see what her mother was holding. "It's Thomas," she said, surprised.

Marie was confused. Why was she carrying Thomas out to the ocean? Then it dawned on her as Frances bent down over the water. "Mother!" she screamed as she got up and ran over to the shore.

Anna followed her, but didn't quite realize what was happening. Then as the girls came closer they saw their brother lying on the sand as the waves lapped at his legs. "Mama, no!" Anna shrieked.

"Mother, don't!" Marie gave a bloodcurdling scream.

Meanwhile, in one of the upstairs bedrooms, Edward was on the verge of sleep when he heard the screams. He jumped up and clumsily got out of bed. He looked out the window, but could not get a clear view. He put his shoes on as fast as he could, then ran down the stairs. As he made his way out the door, he could see his daughters grabbing at their mother. He ran over to them, his daughters' screams getting louder as he approached. Margaret and Harry had also heard the screams and came running out.

"What's going on?" Edward yelled as he clumsily made his way down the rocks and onto the beach.

"She put Thomas in the ocean!" Anna yelled.

"We can't find him!" Marie shouted as she trudged into the waves.

"What!" Edward yelled desperately. He ran to his wife and roughly grabbed her arms. "What did you do to him?" he screamed at her. "Where is he?"

The woman just stared ahead of her. She didn't look at him, her face a blank slate with a drowsy look in her eyes. "I had to give him to the sea." Her voice was distant.

He shook her again. "I could kill you!" he screamed through gritted teeth. He roughly let go of her and began to frantically search for his child. "Thomas!" he cried out. He waded into the waves in a frenzy, grasping into the water to feel if his son had gone under.

Margaret came to Frances's side. "My God, woman," she spoke hurriedly and angrily. "You must truly be mad to kill your own child!" Her Irish brogue came off thick then. She pushed past Frances and began to look for the baby.

Frances just stood there, her gaze fixed on some random point in the distance. "I had to give him to the sea," she repeated.

The five others were searching for the baby, but they could find him nowhere; not in the water, on the beach, or on the rocks. Edward was nearing a state of hysteria by this point, on the verge of injuring himself in his search for the boy. "Thomas!" he screamed. "Where is my son?"

☙

From the far side of the rocks, keeping herself invisible with the help of her powers, stood the siren. Her violet eyes watched the scene before her. She hummed a quiet, gentle tune, soothing the child in her arms, putting him to sleep. Keeping him close to her chest, she rocked him gently. He was a beautiful little boy, she had to admit. She wanted to keep him; she could feed off his energy for years since he was so young.

"Thomas!" The boy's father's screams were heart-wrenching.

She looked down at the baby in her arms. "Why would a mother want to give away such a beautiful child?" she whispered partly to herself, partly to the baby in her arms. It was a puzzling scene to watch as the mother set her child down in the waves. The siren had immediately hummed a sweet tune to have the waves come her way and bring her the baby. She picked the drenched little one out of the water and tried to understand what had possessed Frances to do such a thing, although she had a very good idea.

The siren looked up again. Edward was desperately searching for the boy, his face contorted into absolute despair. She couldn't help but feel sorrow for the man. *How miserable it must be to lose one of your children; one of the only things in the world worth living for*, she thought. She looked down at the baby, at his beautiful sleeping face. It would be hell for a man never knowing what his son would grow up to be like.

It was then that she realized she couldn't do it. She could not take his child away, especially after how much she had taunted him. It would be cruel to take his son away, too cruel even for her. She gently placed the child down on the rocks and slowly backed away from him. When she was far enough away, the child began to cry. He was in unknown surroundings and he was scared. He was wet from the water that he had been in and he was crying for warmth. His cries grew louder and louder.

❧

Edward looked up and turned immediately when he heard the cries. He ran in their direction and a great relief passed over him. He found his son kicking and crying on one of the rocks and immediately picked him up. He held the child tightly to his chest and kissed his head repeatedly.

"Oh thank God!" he whispered, as tears fell from his eyes. "Thank God."

The others came rushing over and all breathed a sigh of relief to see that the baby was perfectly okay.

"Harry," he said gruffly, tears welling up in his throat. "Take Frances inside. Make sure she stays in the parlor."

The older man nodded and did as he was told. Edward got up from his kneeling position and looked his son over, making sure he was not injured. He started to turn and head back to the keeper's quarters when he caught a brief glimpse of the siren before she faded from view. He paused for a moment, but then continued on his way to the house. He went up to his bedroom, where he and Margaret dried Thomas off and put him in fresh clothes. After the baby was changed and checked for injuries, Edward held him for a long time, afraid to ever let him go.

❧

The tension in the parlor was thick as Edward finally confronted a crying Frances, who had seemingly regained her senses. She was too afraid to look at him and he was doing all he could to contain his anger. Harry stood in the corner, having stood guard to make sure the woman didn't leave the room.

"What the fuck were you thinking?" Edward asked tersely.

She flinched, never having heard him speak to her with such language before. Her jaw quivered as she shook her head. "Is he... is he alright?" was her meek response.

"Yes, no thanks to you," he snapped. "I can't believe you did this. But I'm not surprised; you've hated him since the day he was born."

Frances looked up through tears. "No... no." She shook her head. "It was the voices... they told me to do it, they wouldn't stop."

"Voices?" He sighed before continuing, "This can't go on." She nodded. "I'm going to pack your things; you're leaving."

"Where... where are you sending me?" Her eyes grew wide with fright, fearing he would send her to an asylum.

"To Augusta," he said quietly. Her heart sank.

"No, Edward, please don't, please!" she pleaded with him.

"I don't have a choice, Frances, you've left me with no other options," he said half-heartedly. He didn't want to send her to the asylum, but that was before the events of today.

"Can't you send me to my sister?"

"Why, so you can hurt her children?" His words stung as if he had slapped her. "They cannot handle your condition. None of us have the skills nor the proper equipment to help you. It's safer for you and everyone else if you are at the hospital."

"You're going to leave me there." Her body racked with sobs. "You're going to abandon me."

"I'm not abandoning you," he explained. "I'll be able to see you any time and you won't be there forever. Just long enough for you to get better."

"Edward, please," she begged. "Don't you know what they do to people in those places?"

He turned from her. "I'm going upstairs to pack your things," he stated and left the room. This was the end of the discussion as far as he was concerned. Indeed, he had heard stories about the mistreatment and neglect of patients in asylums, but Dr. Neumann assured him that the hospital in Augusta was one of the better establishments. Still, he had never seen the place for himself, but he had no choice at this point. Despite his reservations, he knew this was the last chance she had for improvement.

Frances sat stunned. She turned to Harry, hoping for some sort of relief, but received none. Tears poured forth from her eyes in a violent stream. She felt unbearably alone and like the world had turned against her. But mostly, she felt a horrific guilt for what she had done. The voices wouldn't stop. They kept taunting her to take Thomas to the waves, and she finally snapped. In that moment she thought if she just gave them what they wanted, they would leave her alone. She barely even remembered taking her son outside and to the beach as her mind had been in a fog. But now that clarity had returned, the self-loathing washed over her. How could she have done it? She should have been stronger than this, but she just wasn't. It was like something had taken over her and she couldn't fight it.

Edward stopped when he got to the top of the stairs and saw his girls standing there. They were holding onto each other and crying.

"Why did she do it?" Marie sobbed. "Why did she want Thomas to die?"

Edward walked closer to his daughters. "She didn't want him to die," he said quietly. "Your mother is not in her right mind, she didn't know what she was doing."

"Is he alright?" Anna asked.

"He's fine, girls," Edward replied softly.

"Is she going away?" Marie inquired.

Edward nodded. "She needs time to rest and collect herself, but she will come back eventually." However, Edward was not sure he could ever trust his wife around his children again.

꽃

From a distance the Maine Insane Hospital could pass for a stately mansion. It had manicured lawns and gardens leading up to the arched portico and entrance to the hospital. But as one got closer, the grayish-white building looked more utilitarian and prisonlike. Frances was shaking the entire time as Edward led her up to the admissions wing. He had the medical certificate from Dr. Colson and Dr. Neumann about her condition and the commitment papers from the Port DePaix municipal court. He had been so sure about this, but now his stomach was turning as they got closer to the entrance. But he had to remind himself that he could no longer provide for her and these people could.

Frances stopped dead as they approached the door. "Please, I'll be good, I won't do it again, I promise."

"Frances, it's not that simple and you can't be

certain you wouldn't do it again," he said, finding it hard to look into her eyes. He placed a hand on her back and forced her to keep moving. Once inside, they made their way over to the admissions desk.

"How can I help you today?" one of the attendants greeted, looking between them.

"I need to admit my wife," Edward replied with embarrassment.

"What is her condition?" the admissions officer asked.

"She has been suffering from puerperal insanity. That's what her alienist diagnosed her with," Edward explained.

"And how long has she been in treatment with him?" the man inquired.

"For about a month or so now, but she…" He breathed deeply before continuing, "She tried to kill our son."

The attendant nodded solemnly. "I understand. Do you have her papers?" Edward handed him the commitment papers and the man looked them over. Then he took some papers and a pencil and handed them to Edward. "Please answer these questions so we can admit her."

He took a seat and began to fill out the forms. Frances didn't look at him, feeling sick to her stomach. She looked around at the hospital and started to cry. The walls were stark white with no ornamentation except for the oak woodwork. She was going to have to get used to these walls for they were going to be her home indefinitely. After Edward filled out the paperwork, a nurse came over to speak with them and Edward gave her the details of Frances's condition. They assigned her a room and led her to it.

"You'll have to share a room," the nurse stated. "Too many patients for single rooms. Dr. Thornton will be in shortly to speak with you."

Fear suddenly filled Frances. She had no idea who this roommate would be and if she would be dangerous. And what would this doctor have to say? She was grateful that the bedding and the furniture seemed clean at least. Edward placed her valise on a chair in the room as Frances sat on the bed. She hunched over and began to sob. The bed dipped down next to her as Edward sat down. He placed an arm around her shoulders.

"Please, I'm sorry. I'll be good," she cried. "Please, take me home!"

"Frances, you know I can't," he sighed. "I wish I could snap my fingers and make all of this go away, but I can't. You need help and this is where you will get it."

After several moments, Dr. Thornton came to the room and examined her. He talked at length about the treatment she would be given there and what her chances were for improvement. When he left, Edward offered her some advice and assurances.

"Look at me," he said. Reluctantly she looked into his eyes. "You have to try really hard to get better. You have to be willing to work with the doctors and the staff."

"And if I don't get better I'll never see you or my children again," she grumbled.

"Stop thinking like that," he asserted. "What happened to that strong woman I married?"

"She's gone," Frances whispered.

"No she isn't," he declared. "She *is* in there and you need to find her again. That Frances would never give up. She would fight like hell to get home to her family. Be that fighter again. I know you can."

She shook her head. "I feel like I have no fight left in me."

"That fire is in there; you just have to believe it. You'll get through this because you are strong, even if you don't think you are. And you will see us all again." He kissed her head. "I'll come to visit you often, I promise."

He left her then and she felt both angry and hurt. She couldn't help but feel anger at her husband for leaving her here and seemingly giving up on helping her, despite whatever reassurances he tried to give her. But there was also the painful reminder that she deserved this. She did the unthinkable and knew she couldn't be trusted around her family anymore. But she resolved to herself that she would get better and she would get back to her family. She would find her strength and be a fighter once again.

˃

Edward sat in the watch room with Harry that night. He mostly looked out the window and didn't say much. Harry would occasionally look up at him and consider saying something before deciding to just keep quiet.

It was Edward who finally broke the silence. "Do you think…" He had trouble getting the words out. "Do you think I've really lost her?"

Harry considered for a moment. "I can't say honestly," he finally answered. "This is a hard thing to come back from. Hopefully the hospital will be able to set her straight."

"She was never like this." Edward shook his head. "Even after her miscarriage, she wasn't like this. It got worse after Thomas."

"People sometimes go through things like this," Harry offered, pausing before continuing, "Did I ever tell you about Crazy Al?"

"No," Edward replied, but he didn't really care to hear it.

"When I was in the Navy, we were lucky to get some time off one day while our ship was in port. A lot of us chose to go ashore," he said. "I went to one of the makeshift hospitals on the mainland. I had heard one of my friends was there, so I wanted to visit him. God, I'll never forget the things I saw in that hospital. Grown, strong men crying out in agony, most of 'em with limbs missing. And the stench! Have you ever smelt death?"

Edward just shook his head.

"It's a smell I'll never forget." Harry got a distant look in his eyes. "I went all around that hospital searching for my friend and I finally found him. He never looked at me, he never said anything to me, just stared ahead into nothingness. He wasn't there. I don't know where he was, but he wasn't there. I was going to leave when he wouldn't respond to me, but then I heard yelling from behind me. When I looked, one of the men had grabbed the surgeon's saw and was running around with it, swatting it all around him. One of his arms was missing and he kept yelling 'They're coming! They're coming!' I don't know who *they* were, but he was terrified of them and he was trying to get them away from him."

"Did they get him to stop?" Edward asked.

"That was the strangest part," he replied. "My

friend suddenly woke up out of his stupor and cracked him over the head, knocked him out cold. 'That's Crazy Al,' he told me. 'Goddamn son-of-a-bitch. He's always yelling; always trying to remind the rest of us of the horror.' Then my friend lay back down and went back into his stupor. I heard some years later, they put old Al into an asylum. He somehow managed to grab one of the surgeons' scalpels and cut his own throat with it after stabbing a doctor."

"Well, that certainly makes me feel optimistic," Edward grunted under his breath.

"But that's not all," Harry continued. "I saw my friend again a few years later. He was doing better. He had managed to marry his sweetheart and she told me that he sometimes still woke up with nightmares. Last I saw him was at a mutual friend's funeral. He was completely normal, but I'll never forget that stare of his. And I hate to say it, but it was the same one your wife had earlier."

Edward quietly asked, "So what's your point?"

"That Frances can end up like Crazy Al or like my friend," he said nonchalantly. "There's hope for her still; just have to keep on praying everything turns out alright."

Edward said nothing the rest of the night and resumed looking out the window. He heard the siren singing again. He wanted so badly to confront her about any part she had in his wife's attempted infanticide, but he was too exhausted to move and certainly too exhausted to fight the woman off. And he really didn't want to recall the day's events.

CHAPTER 11- BANDITS AND SPIRITS

Edward came down from the light early the next morning. The sunlight was nearly unbearable on his eyes. He mentally cursed himself for looking out at the ocean. The waves glistened in the morning sun and the glare hurt his eyes. He looked toward the rocks and saw her. She was sitting on a large rock, her back to him. She wasn't singing this time. He was surprised that she showed herself in the daylight.

Every fiber in his being was telling him not to, but he slowly walked over to her, keeping a tight hold on the knife in his pocket. She never turned around and her head was down. He wasn't sure if she was looking at something or possibly sleeping. Now in the sunlight he could clearly make out her features more. Her arms were lightly speckled with small, translucent feathers. They continued down her legs where they were more opaque as the cold water lapped at her calves.

"So did you have anything to do with it?" he finally asked, but it came out more tired and less angry than he meant.

"No," she replied simply.

"Then why were you there?" he asked.

"I pulled him out of the waves," she stated, a bitter edge to her voice.

"So you saved him?" The sarcasm was evident in his tone. "I would find it much more convincing if you said you had manipulated my wife into drowning him."

"I could have taken him for myself, I could have killed him, just like your wife had planned, of which I had no part in," she said with venom in her voice, finally turning to give him a deathly glare, "but I gave him back to you." Even with the anger in her eyes, she was stunningly beautiful.

"So am I supposed to thank you for not kidnapping or killing my son?" he scoffed.

"Careful now," she said quietly. "I did one good deed; I may just have to make up for it with a bad one."

He returned her glare. "If you hurt anyone in my household…"

"You'll do what? Kill me?" she laughed. "I'm immortal; you couldn't kill me if you tried. Although, I suppose I wouldn't mind if you did…" She muttered the last part and looked away.

He found the statement odd and confusing. "Fine, I'll humor you," he relented. "Why did you save my son?"

"A brief moment of compassion, I suppose." She shrugged.

"Compassion?" he asked suspiciously. "That sounds odd coming from you."

"When you've been alone for as long as I have,

sometimes you do not wish the same fate on others." Her tone became sad. She got up and started to walk away.

He was utterly confounded by her sudden change in demeanor. "You're an odd woman," he said.

She turned back slowly. "I have a name," she spoke softly. "It's Elysia."

☙

Willie sighed as he leaned back against the brick wall. "He said he'd be here by now."

"Probably late on purpose; doesn't want to look suspicious," Bert replied.

The two men were standing in a dingy alleyway a few towns over waiting for their long-time friend and partner to show up. They were of different height and build. Willie had blue eyes brighter than a summer sky and wilder than a raging bull, making it impossible to guess what he would do next. His normally sandy-blond curls were now shortly cropped on his head and he had his hat pulled down low over his face to try and hide it. Bert was letting his brown hair grow out as well as his beard and mustache. It was uncomfortable, but necessary to keep people from recognizing them from the police sketches that were being passed around.

After a few more moments passed, a man in a lounge suit walked up to the edge of the alleyway. He turned his back and pulled out his watch. He made sure no one was around before heading into the alley.

"You two are going to be the death of me," Howard Martin of the East Knox Insurance Company sighed as he walked up to Bert and Willie.

"Do you two realize the mess you've made?"

"Well, nice to see you too, Howard," Bert scoffed.

"What the hell is wrong with you two? Why didn't you stick to the plan?" Howard asked.

"Just what are you on about?" Willie asked in return.

"The *Josephine*," he replied. "Murdering the crew and taking its cargo weren't part of the plan."

"Well, maybe Cassinger shouldn't be so fucking greedy then," Willie countered. "We're the ones sticking our necks out here, doing all the dirty work, while he reaps all the rewards sitting at his fucking desk. We just wanted to get our rightful share."

"Your *rightful share* cost us our whole operation, idiots," Howard snapped. "You've got local law enforcement looking into this, the people over at the insurance company, and the Revenue Cutter Service, which might I remind you is part of the federal fucking government. What I'm trying to say is: you've become a liability. We had to sabotage a ship insured with another company just to throw them all off course."

"What are you talking about?"

"A ship suffered an explosion in the waters off Wawenock Point a few nights ago," he explained casually. "I'm surprised you didn't hear about it. The papers have been selling it as another USS *Maine*."

"Think we care about reading the papers?" Willie asked.

"You should, considering you're the front page news." Martin raised an eyebrow. "And what happened to Tim?"

"He left us." Willie shrugged. "Decided to go his

own way."

Howard just stared at him. "You really are dumb. Guess you didn't hear about how he washed up dead on shore?"

"We had nothing to do with that!" Bert was quick to defend them.

"Then I suppose he cut his own throat after successfully robbing the *Josephine* clean?" Martin quirked an eyebrow. "Jesus, have you been hiding under a rock or do you just take me for a fool?"

Willie's eyes grew dark as he huffed, "He was growing soft. He didn't want to keep going… and he was threatening to turn us in."

"You had to kill him though? He's been our friend since we were children." Martin shook his head. "I feel like I don't even know you two anymore."

"Well, that's not surprising," Bert chimed in. "You sit up in your fancy office, making a decent wage, while we're out here trying to survive on crumbs."

"It's not my fault you decided to keep living a life of crime."

"Oh, don't act so innocent," Willie snarled. "You used to go around town with us robbing the local stores. I remember Old Man Jackson used to chase us down the block."

"Oh, for God's sake!" Martin shouted. "That was a long time ago. We were just kids then. I've put that behind me."

"And now you're onto insurance fraud," Bert stated.

"*Was*," Martin corrected. "I think it's needless to say at this point that we're stopping the operation. It's getting too risky now. Cassinger and the ship owners are getting nervous."

"They're the ones who wanted to wreck their own ships," Bert stated. "They thought they were worth more destroyed than operational."

"I know that," Martin said. "But that was before the *Josephine* debacle and the authorities figuring us out."

"And what about me and Bert?" Willie asked. "What are we supposed to do?"

"Cassinger and I have decided that it would be best to settle this matter practically than to have any of our heads on the chopping block," Martin explained. "We want you two to get out of Maine, make for New York or further south if you can."

"Now you want to tell us where to live?"

"You really can't stay here with everyone looking for you, now can you?" Howard asked rhetorically. "Think of it as a fresh start. Really, you should be grateful. It's the best option you have."

"This is bullshit!" Willie roared. "You use us and then just discard us."

"You got your money and whatever valuables you stole from the *Josephine*," he reminded them. "Now take what's left of your lives and get out of here before you find yourselves dead or behind bars."

"Just who the hell do you think you are?" Willie yelled in Martin's face. "You really forgot where you came from, you know that?" Bert held him back as he shoved Martin.

"If it weren't for me, Cassinger would've put you both in an early grave!" Martin fumed.

That made Bert and Willie stop. "He wanted to kill us?" Bert looked at him incredulously.

"He thought you being dead would be safer than if you got caught and started to talk," Martin explained. "But I pleaded with him to just let you run."

"That son-of-a-bitch," Willie murmured.

"He had a point, I'll admit." Martin snorted. "But it would've just raised more questions. So I think you two should just make a run for it before he changes his mind."

Willie and Bert turned to each other for a moment, considering. "Listen, there are wanted posters for us everywhere," Bert said. "I don't know about you, but I'd rather not end up back in jail, or worse, dead. Let's take the money we saved and get out. There isn't anything in this state for us anyway."

Willie stared at him for a bit before finally sighing and relenting. "Fine, we can start our own damn operation. Probably more money out in New York anyway."

"You can do whatever the hell you want, just don't do it here," Martin told them.

"We don't need you anyway." Willie sneered at him. "Forget we even existed."

"Gladly," Howard shot back. Willie glared at him before he and Bert walked away.

꙳

Edward went to Frances's family in town and told them what happened. Frances's sister, Carrie, and her husband, Frank, were both home and, unfortunately, Frances's father, Phillip, was there as well paying a visit. It was not the type of news any of them were expecting. When they were sitting in the parlor,

Edward described the events. Carrie became upset as Edward related the details. Phillip was quietly fuming.

"But I thought she was seeing a doctor," Carrie said.

"I took her to an alienist, Dr. Neumann, and he gave her a treatment regimen," Edward explained. "She tried it for some time, but all it seemed to do was make her sleep more, nothing else."

"How... how was she after...well, after what she tried to do?" Carrie couldn't bring herself to speak of the attempted infanticide.

"After we saved Thomas, I think she finally realized what she did and she just kept crying. But she revealed to me that she had been hearing voices telling her to do it," Edward stated. "She never said anything to me about it before then, nor did she tell Dr. Neumann."

"Oh God, Edward." Carrie started crying. "It was really that bad?" Edward just nodded.

Frank spoke up at this point. "Did you go into the asylum with her?" Edward nodded again. "What was it like?"

"It seemed like a good, clean facility," Edward claimed. "There were a lot of patients from what I could see, but Dr. Neumann assured me the staff was good."

"Well, of course he wouldn't say anything bad about them," Phillip finally chimed in. "He's probably friends with all of them. Why didn't you consult with us first?"

"It's not like I had time to pay you all a visit," Edward explained. "She tried to murder our son. I was scared of what she would do next."

"She shouldn't have gotten pregnant again." Carrie shook her head. "She wasn't ready for it."

Edward felt his throat clench. The thought had crossed his mind several times already. "We thought it would help her; relieve her of the pain after her miscarriage."

"No, *you* thought it would help her." Phillip glared at him. "You pushed her into it."

The way his words echoed Frances's own stung Edward. "She *agreed* to it," he hissed. "And no one could have foreseen this illness falling upon her."

The father continued to grumble, "My daughter should have never married you. I always knew she could do better than some lowly lightkeeper."

"You didn't say that when we were first married!" Edward snapped. "You used to praise me for being such a hardworking, honest man."

"That's before you turned on her," he said. "You let her go insane and then you dropped her off at some hellhole. I should go retrieve her myself!"

"Then go ahead! Take her out of the asylum and run the risk of her attempting to murder one of you!" Edward roared. "I have three children. She tried to kill one of them. Do you really think I was just going to let her try to kill the other two?"

That shut the man up. Carrie and Frank were also taken aback. Edward took a deep breath. "My children are everything to me," he said softly. "I wouldn't let anyone hurt them, not even their mother."

"But did you really have to take her there?" Carrie asked gently.

"I didn't know what else to do. I wasn't able to help her anymore." Edward shook his head. "I'm hoping they're able to. It's my last hope." His shoulders sank. "And I'm going to visit her often to see how she's progressing and to make sure she isn't being mistreated."

"We'll go see her too." Carrie turned to her husband. "She'll need company being all alone in that place."

"I think she'd appreciate that," Edward stated. "She often said she missed you, even though I offered to take her to go see you several times."

"Well, that's my fault too. I should have visited her," Carrie said as a few tears fell. "And if it's alright with you, I'd like to come over maybe once a week or so to help with the house and the children."

"Oh no, I wouldn't want to put you out of your way." Edward waved his hand.

"Really, it's no trouble," Carrie said. "They are my family too."

"I know and thank you." He stood up then. "I really must be going. I'll keep you informed as to her condition and when she will be expected home."

"Yes, please do," Carrie urged as she led him to the front door. "I'd like to be there to welcome her home."

~

Marie was cleaning up her father's office that afternoon. She was still shaken from the previous day's events. She mindlessly swept the floor as her thoughts wandered to her mother. Part of her was so angry at her mother for trying to kill her beloved brother, but another part of her was just upset and confused. She knew her mother had been in a deep melancholy, but she never knew it was that bad.

The idea of her mother being gone also saddened her. She didn't know how long she would be away or if she would ever come home. She also wondered if she would ever go back to the way she was. A silent tear fell from her eye and she gently brushed it off. She tried to choke back the rest of her tears as they threatened to fall from her red-rimmed eyes.

She continued sweeping the floor and was trying to get the dust out from behind one of the cabinets when the broom hit something. Stopping, she looked and saw a rectangular object wedged between the cabinet and wall. She dug the object out as scraps of yellowed paper fell from it. The object was a sort of portfolio, and upon opening it Marie saw the old newspaper clippings it held.

She had no idea why the portfolio was there or who had saved the clippings. She doubted that it was her father, as many of the clippings were from before they had moved to the keeper's quarters. They went as far back as the 1830s, before the light was even built. She looked through many of them; some were about shipwrecks and their victims, others more sinister, about murders and such. Still many more were on mundane topics such as new inventions or political events.

She continued to skim through them, being careful not to rip the delicate, crinkled paper. She stopped at one dated 1874, not long after the lighthouse had been built. Her heart stopped as she looked at the yellowed clipping. The headline read "Lightkeeper's Children Found Drowned." But it wasn't the headline that caught her interest, it was the black-and-white pictures that accompanied it. They were of a little boy and girl. The caption beneath read, "James, 9, and Louise, 12. The children of Mr. Fredrick Varner."

Louise? Marie thought to herself. *Is this the same Louise who tried to get me to come to the cave?*

It wasn't possible, it just wasn't. A chill crept up her spine and she was frozen in place. She dared to read through the rest of the article: "The children were playing on the rocks when a storm began. It is likely the sudden large waves overcame the children and led to their untimely passing."

Playing on the rocks, Marie thought as realization struck her hard. *The cave, they were in the cave.* And they had wanted her and her sister to go into that cave. Suddenly, Madame Leonora's words rang through her mind once more. *Be wary of the spirits that haunt the shores of the light.*

CHAPTER 12- GHOSTS REVEALED

The next day Marie sat at the window looking at her sister in the front yard. Anna was aimlessly running around trying to catch butterflies, having already moved on from the magic tricks. Daisy was close behind her, apparently wanting to join in the game. She shook her head. Anna was too reckless, too trusting. Marie had to warn her. She went outside, trying to walk quickly to her sister without breaking into a run.

"Anna!" she called.

"What?" her sister asked, annoyed, not stopping her little game.

"I need to speak with you," Marie said, stopping in the middle of the lawn.

"Not now! I'm busy!" Anna yelled as she continued her fun.

"This is serious! Come here!" Marie commanded.

"Oh fine," Anna huffed and walked over to her sister. "What is it?"

"You can't play with Louise and Jimmy

anymore," Marie stated firmly.

"Why?" Anna cried. "I know Louise upset you, but if you would only come and play with us…"

"Anna, they're dangerous! They'll hurt you!" Marie cut her sister off. "Never ever play with them again!"

"You can't make me! They're my friends! They won't hurt me!" Anna yelled back.

"They're not your friends!" Marie shouted. She had hoped she wouldn't have to tell her the truth, but her sister was stubborn beyond belief. She hesitated before continuing, "Anna they're spirits; they have been dead for years."

Anna just stared at her for a moment then finally asked, "Do you think I'll fall for that?"

Marie sighed and pulled the newspaper clipping from her pinafore and showed it to Anna. Anna took her time reading it over, trying to understand all the words, and her face contorted in shock. She grew pale and slowly looked up at her sister, her eyes wide with fright.

"No…" she whispered. She began shaking her head violently. "It can't be true. Where did you get this?"

"In Father's office," Marie answered. "There was a whole folder filled with old newspapers."

Tears fell from her sister's eyes and she threw herself into a panic. "This isn't happening! I'm scared!" she wailed. "I played with them for so long and never knew! They'll want me to go back to the cave with them!"

"Do not go," Marie said sternly. "No matter what, do not go with them."

Anna shook her head and then threw her arms

around Marie, her tears soaking Marie's pinafore.

☙

Edward was walking down the hall from his room, ready to take up his post in the watch room that night, when he saw a light coming from his daughters' room. It was odd that they should still be up at this hour. He gently rapped on the door before slowly opening it. He saw Marie staring out the window. Anna was sleeping on the opposite side of the room, the blankets pulled up over her head despite the heat.

"Marie, dear, it's late, why are you still up?" he asked gently.

"I can't sleep," she replied quietly, not turning from the window.

"Why? Had a bad dream?" He walked into the room.

"No," she said.

He sighed. "Is it about your mother?"

"No," she said again and was silent for a moment before nearly whispering, "You wouldn't believe me…"

He almost didn't hear it, it was so soft. "Try me," he coaxed, sitting down on the edge of her bed.

She slowly turned around. She had dark circles under her eyes and the weariest of faces. "I can't tell you." She looked down. "I just can't because I know you won't believe me. You'll think I'm telling stories."

"You may be surprised at what I'll believe," he said, considering all of the strange things he had witnessed.

Marie thought for a moment, then sat on the bed

opposite him. "Anna met these two children," she explained, a somber tone to her voice. "She plays with them in the cave that's behind the lighthouse."

"There's no cave here," he corrected, raising an eyebrow curiously.

"That's what I used to think," Marie said, looking down at the blankets. "But there is; I've seen it."

Edward was surprised by this information. "You'll have to show me one day."

"No!" Marie exclaimed, looking up at him with wide, fearful eyes. "I will never go back there. Not after what I found out about those two children."

"What children? Who's been coming here?" Edward asked, worry setting in. "Are they mean? Did they hurt you?"

Marie just stared for a moment before reaching over to her nightstand and pulling out the newspaper clipping from inside one of her books. She handed it to her father. He read it over carefully.

"Where did you find this?" he inquired.

"It was in a folder in your office with a bunch of other newspapers," she answered. "I found it when I was cleaning."

"Strange, I've never seen that in there before," he said. "But are you trying to tell me that these are the two children Anna has been playing with?"

Marie looked down again. "I knew you wouldn't believe me."

"Well, it is a bit hard to believe, that these two children are spirits," he stated matter-of-factly. "But that doesn't mean it's not true."

Marie looked up in shock. "You do believe me?"

"Let's just say I've had similar experiences."

Marie was confused. "But what do I do about

them?" she asked. "I'm afraid they'll hurt us, especially after what Madame Leonora told us."

Edward knitted his eyebrows. "Who's that?"

"She's a fortune teller on the boardwalk," Marie answered. "The day Margaret took us there she came up to Anna and me. She said, 'I see a darkness invading your life. Be wary of the spirits that haunt the shores of the light.'"

"She shouldn't have scared you like that," he said sternly, annoyed that a stranger would frighten his children.

"I know, but I think she wanted to warn us," she explained.

"I might just need to have a word with her," he said. "But until then, you sleep. You and Anna stay away from any spirit children in the meantime and let me know if you see them again. And say your prayers; God will protect you."

She nodded and lay down in bed. He kissed her forehead before leaving the room. He would indeed speak with this Leonora, but it was also for his own curiosity. He too had seen strange things and wanted answers.

※

It was a hot morning when Edward decided to go to the boardwalk in search of Madame Leonora. He didn't believe in these so-called fortune tellers, but maybe, just maybe, this woman wasn't a fraud. After all, how would she have known that the two girls she spoke to were the same ones who inhabited the keeper's quarters at Wawenock Point?

He walked along the boardwalk and came up to a

small shop that had the words "Madame Leonora" painted on its façade. He walked inside to a small table with all sorts of strange objects on it. The room was heavily embellished with dark blue velvet curtains. A woman with dark hair and eyes walked out from behind the curtains. She was dressed in a plain white shirtwaist and an A-line, gored skirt, atypical of her usual garb that she put on for effect. She was startled to see Edward there.

"Oh, sir, I'm sorry, but I'm closed," she said meekly.

"I'm not here for you to tell me my fortune," he said. "My name is Edward Ashman. I'm a keeper at the Wawenock Point Lighthouse."

Realization spread across the woman's face. She knew why he was here. "Oh, is that so," she said, pretending to be ignorant.

"I don't know if you remember, but a few weeks ago you spoke to two little girls," he said in a stern tone. "You were telling them something about some spirits or other. Those two girls were my daughters."

The woman stood up straighter, her face becoming more serious. "Yes, I spoke to your daughters. I needed to warn them."

"I don't appreciate you scaring them," he reprimanded her.

"I had to," she said matter-of-factly. "It was the only way for them to listen."

"What did you mean by it?" he asked.

"I meant that there are many souls around the shores of the lighthouse," she said solemnly. "Many are angry and dangerous."

"Yes, and you know this because you can see the future," he said cynically, testing the woman's claims.

"Funny, I could have taken you for a fraud. What is it with people nowadays and their desire to be fooled by supernatural spectacles?"

"I am not a fraud," she fumed.

"And I suppose your name is really Leonora too." He smirked.

She turned her head. "It's Eleanor," she muttered.

"So Eleanor rearranged becomes Leonora," a small laugh coming from his throat. "How original."

"I thought it was clever," she growled. "But I am not a fraud."

"So you take people's money honestly?" he asked.

"Look, I will admit I may embellish the truth a bit when it comes to my business"—he rolled his eyes at that—"but I do see things. I have visions. When I dream I can see things that have yet to come, things that have already passed, and I saw a vision about your girls."

"And what exactly did you see?" he asked, giving her a chance to explain herself.

"I saw two dark shadows luring them beneath the earth." Her words froze his blood. "There was nothing but darkness. And I saw a shadow bringing a small child to the ocean."

He was silent, a chill creeping up his spine. It all fell into place: the Varner children, the cave Marie mentioned, the voices his wife claimed told her to kill their son. "You were sure they were the same children?" he asked.

"I couldn't remember their faces all too well," she explained. "But I saw the lighthouse. That was clear. And its light was shining so intensely, like a fire blazing against the night sky. I talked to Mr. Tully; he pointed out your daughters to me."

"Oh, so Walt was in on it," he said.

"I helped him a few years ago with a spiritually related problem of his own," she told him. "I have his confidence."

"What do these spirits want?" he asked, afraid of the answer.

"I am not exactly sure," she said. "But I assure you it is nothing good." She observed his tenseness carefully. "I have a feeling you've had an encounter of your own with them."

"Just one," he admitted, a little surprised with his honesty.

"She's an ancient spirit," she said. Edward immediately perked at her recognition of the siren. "Yes, I saw her too."

"What do I do about her?" he asked, curious about what she'd say.

"I don't think there is anything you can do," she replied. "But oddly enough, I didn't have the same sinister feelings with her as I did with the other spirits I saw. I only felt loneliness."

"She did claim to save my son, but I don't think I can believe her," he said quietly, puzzled by this new information.

"I don't know." She gave him a sympathetic look. "But I know that you and your family should leave that place before it's too late."

CHAPTER 13- A STORM GATHERS

Anna was shaky after finding out that information about Louise and Jimmy. She refused to even go outside. She stayed in the house doing chores and would jump every so often when she heard a noise. The day had mostly been quiet until right before supper. Then she saw them through the window.

Jimmy was beckoning her to come with them. Anna just froze, breath catching in her throat. She was about to run out of the room when she heard Louise's voice. "Won't you come outside?" she asked.

"No!" Anna shouted. "Go away!"

"Why don't you want to play with us anymore?" Jimmy asked.

"I bet it's that sister of yours filling your head up with bad things," Louise said.

"The only thing she fills my head up with is the truth!" Anna retorted. "Now leave me alone!"

"You'll have to come back to us eventually," Jimmy sneered.

Anna turned around and covered her ears and

shut her eyes. "Go away!"

"What's the matter with you?" Anna looked up to see Margaret in front of her with her hands on her hips. She had one eyebrow raised, a look of annoyance on her face.

"Uh...nothing," Anna mumbled, her eyes growing wide and her cheeks flaring red with embarrassment.

"Just get back to your chores," Margaret stated sharply and turned to get back to her own.

Anna dared to look back once more, but Louise and Jimmy were gone. The two had managed to hide themselves behind the corner of the house. They both wore angry expressions.

"Don't worry," Louise said to her brother. "She won't be able to keep away from us forever."

☙

An hour or so before the sun would begin setting, Bert and Willie rowed their boat through the waters near Wawenock Point. They had taken with them whatever they could and decided to make their way out of Maine. Their plan was to go by boat to the next town over, where Cassinger had told them a captain of a steamer ship who owed him a favor would stow them away in the cargo hold until they reached New York City. They decided that taking a boat to the port would be less risky, as there were too many people likely to identify them at a train station or on the main roads. Of course Willie griped about how they could have just walked there while still avoiding all the main thoroughfares.

"This is a more direct route and there's no one

out here," Bert reminded him. "You're just too lazy to keep rowing."

"My arms are getting tired!" Willie complained. "You and your stupid plans."

Bert just rolled his eyes. Suddenly a tremor shook the small boat and they grabbed onto the sides. "The waves are picking up," Bert commented. He looked up at the sky and saw the dark, threatening clouds. "Looks like a storm is coming, better row faster."

Willie shot him a glare, but did as he was told. Unfortunately, just moments later the sky opened and it began to rain. The waves likewise became more intense and water splashed into the boat.

"We need to stop!" Bert yelled.

"There's a beach up ahead!" Willie called out. "We can stop there!"

With frantic arms, they tried with all their might to reach the small stretch of beach. The waves were pushing back against their efforts, though, and one moved them dangerously close to the rocks.

"Quick, steer that way!" Bert gestured to the left side of the boat.

Their attempts were useless as another large wave slammed them into the cliffs. "Fuck!" Willie cried as he saw that the collision had made a crack in the boat and it was now filling with water.

"To hell with it!" Bert called. "Let's just get out!"

They grabbed the two small bags they had brought with them and jumped out of the boat and onto the rocks. They climbed up the cliff to get out of the water and stopped to catch their breath.

"Now what do we do?" Willie asked.

"There's a forest over there," Bert observed. "We can wait out the storm there."

"And get soaked in the meantime," Willie grumbled. "There's a lighthouse here. Aren't they supposed to help shipwrecked people? We can just tell them we were sailing when we got caught in the storm and need shelter until it clears up."

"Are you stupid?" Bert asked. "They could recognize us from the wanted posters."

Willie let out a growl. "Forest it is then."

They walked along the rocky coast, trying to make their way to the forest. Willie stopped when he heard wind whistling. He turned and observed the rocks they were standing on. He motioned for Bert. "Help me move this rock."

"Why?" Bert raised an eyebrow.

"I think there might be a cave here," he explained. "We can wait out the storm there."

"Really?" Bert came over and helped to push the thin slab of rock aside.

Sure enough, a narrow, short entrance appeared in the rock face.

"Well I'll be damned." Bert stared, amazed. "You think it's deep enough?" He couldn't quite make out the inside of the cave with the dark clouds blocking out the sun.

"One way to find out." Willie stooped down low and turned sideways to maneuver himself into the cave.

Bert followed suit. Once inside, they tried to make out their surroundings with what little light there was in the day shining through the opening in the cave. Bert looked over the various bottles. "What the hell is all this?"

"You think someone else is already living in here?" Willie asked.

"This close to the lighthouse? Seems risky," Bert said.

They jumped at the sound of a loud thunderclap, which was followed by a groaning sound.

"What was that?" Willie's eyes grew wide as he tried to look deeper into the cave in the dim light.

"Probably just the wind," Bert answered, but even he wasn't sure.

"I heard it again," Willie exclaimed as he tilted his head to listen better.

"Stop being so damned paranoid!" Bert scolded.

"Shh, listen!" Willie hissed. This time what sounded like a man's groan made them both jump up. "I don't think we're alone, Bert."

The sloshing sound of water made them both look at the entrance to the cave. Water started to enter the narrow passageway as the tide rose.

"I think we better get to higher ground," Bert suggested, to which Willie nodded vigorously.

The two scrambled their way out of the cave, nearly knocking each other down in the process. The water lapped at their boots and they stumbled their way over the rocky cliff up to high ground. They started to make their way to the forest when they heard footsteps and a voice: "Hey, you two! Who are you?"

They turned to see a man walking toward them. "Damn, what do we do?" Willie whispered to Bert.

"Play along," Bert whispered back, then shouted to the man. "Oh well, we were just going for a sail, trying to make it back to port. Storm came out of nowhere, caught us off guard."

"The rocks around here and storms don't make for a good pairing, I'm afraid. My name is Edward,

I'm a lightkeeper here. Where's your boat?" Edward asked, walking closer.

"It hit the rocks over there," Willie answered. "She started taking on water."

Edward could just make out the stern of the boat from where he was standing. "We can try to pull it out," he offered

"No, no, it's not worth it," Bert said quickly. "It was old and rotting away anyway. Glad to be rid of it honestly." He and Willie wanted this little exchange to be over with so they could get to the steamer ship.

Edward inquired, "Are you injured?" He looked the men over. They seemed alarmed and flustered, but Edward chalked that up to their accident. Then he frowned as he noticed Willie had a scar on his left cheek. The police sketches of the shipwreckers said one of them had a scar on their face, but Edward couldn't remember if it was the right cheek or the left. These two men only looked vaguely like the sketches, but that was usually par for the course. Still… Edward got goose bumps at the thought.

"No, we're fine," Bert reassured him. "Just wet is all."

"What were you two doing out in the water at this hour anyway?" Edward asked, trying to keep his voice even.

"Just fishing," Willie said, getting into the lie. "We were out all day. We didn't realize how far we drifted out. Then by the time we decided to head back, the storm got us."

"What about your equipment?" Edward asked cautiously.

"We'll just get new nets," Willie stated. "We really should be getting back."

And that's when Edward knew his hunch was correct. Even if their boat was lost, wouldn't they at the very least have tried to save their nets and fishing poles, especially if they had time before the boat sank? "It's a long way back to town," Edward told them, trying to keep them here. "You two should stay here and wait out the storm."

"Thank you, but we wouldn't want to impose." Bert tried to sound polite, while at the same time walking backward a few steps.

"No, I insist. Travelers are welcome here," Edward tried again. "The woods can be dangerous at night and I'll have to write a report about this anyway, so that will take some time."

"Report?" Willie quirked an eyebrow.

"Yes." Edward pointed his thumb back at the lighthouse. "As the head keeper here, I have to report all shipwrecks, no matter how small." He would also be alerting the police about these two.

But before he could do anything, Bert hoisted his bag and smacked Edward in the head with it. When he doubled over in pain and shock, a second blow landed on the back of his head. Edward fell to the ground and the world went black.

"The hell took you so long?" Willie looked at Bert incredulously.

"Well, I didn't see you doing anything."

They pulled the unconscious Edward over to the storage shed. Bert tried the handle and found that it was open. They dragged Edward inside and just as they dropped him off, the door to the storage shed slammed shut. They went to open the door, but it wouldn't budge. Willie pushed against it, to no avail.

"Dammit!" he shouted.

"Try the window," Bert said and they both attempted to open the sole window in the shed. The window was sealed shut and wouldn't open.

"Son-of-a-bitch, what are we going to do now?" Willie was getting nervous.

"There's got to be something in here we can use to pry the door open," Bert said. "Look around."

The two turned their backs and were about to start looking when the door opened. Standing in the doorway was another man, his hunting rifle pointed at the men. "Both of you put your hands up now," he ordered.

"Who the hell are you?" Bert asked in alarm.

"The other keeper," the older man answered. "Now put your damn hands up before I shoot them off."

"Alright, alright, don't go shooting at us." Bert complied, putting his hands up, and Willie followed suit.

"I saw you two knock out my friend here from the window," the man revealed. "Now why would you go and do a thing like that?"

"We just wanted to leave and he wouldn't let us," Willie growled, letting his mouth run off again.

"And where are you off to in such a hurry, especially in this kind of weather?" the keeper asked.

"Ughh, Harry? Is that you?" Edward groaned as he came to.

"It's me, Ed," Harry answered, not taking his eyes off Bert and Willie. "Lay still, son, they did a number on your head. Now answer the damn question."

"I think you got us all wrong," Bert explained. "We just needed to get to the next town to see my mother; she's very ill."

"You needed to see your mother?" Harry raised an eyebrow. "And you come all the way out here?" He shook his head. "No, no, I think you two are on the run. I think you're in a lot of trouble and you needed to get out of town quickly."

"I don't know what you're talking about," Willie rebuffed him.

"Well, I couldn't help but notice that you fit the description of two of the criminals," Harry said. "And you got a scar on your face." He jerked his rifle at Willie. "Just like they said you would."

"You have the wrong men." Bert looked at him straight in the eyes.

"I doubt it."

Edward managed to grapple to his feet, holding his head all the while. He walked over to the rope that was kept in the storage shed and pulled out his pocket knife.

"What are you doing, Ed?" Harry asked. Bert and Willie looked over their shoulders at him.

"Making sure these two don't leave," he replied as he cut two lengths of rope. Then he walked over to Willie. "Put your hands behind your back," Edward commanded.

"Fuck you!" Willie spat at him.

"Do as the man says!" Harry roared.

Bert spotted a heavy-looking lantern out of the corner of his eyes and thought if he could grab it, he could use it to knock Harry out, while Willie got Edward. He made a quick grab for it and Harry shot at him. The bullet grazed his shoulder.

"Holy shit!" Bert cried as he ducked down and grabbed his shoulder. There was a small gash there. The bullet had lodged into the wall of the shed. "You crazy son-of-a-bitch!"

Harry didn't flinch, just got his rifle ready for another shot if needed. "I suggest you do as the man says and put your hands behind your back."

"You're quick for an old man," Willie sneered.

"Quicker than you and not as stupid," Harry shot back. "Now put your hands behind your back and I won't discharge this little lady here again."

Both men did so and allowed Edward to tie their hands. "Are you just going to let me bleed out?" Bert whined.

Edward pulled the man's shirt out of the way to look at the wound. "It's not that deep," he announced.

"See, you'll live," Harry smirked. "Now you two just sit there and be quiet until the police get here. Ed, why don't you go cleanup your head and send Margaret over to the police station? I'll keep an eye on these two," Harry suggested.

"Are you sure?" Edward asked, clutching his head.

Harry nodded. "I don't think these two are going anywhere."

Edward warily walked back to the keeper's quarters. He touched his head again and looked down at his hand to see blood coating it. He walked into the parlor and found Margaret sitting in a chair and reading a book.

"Margaret?" he asked.

She looked up over the top of the book. "What ya want?"

"Can you do me a favor?" he responded, ignoring her tone. "We have a little problem outside."

"What now?" she asked in annoyance.

"We have two men tied up in the storage shed," he explained. "We think they're the two criminals who have been sabotaging all those ships. Harry is keeping guard over them. Can you go into town and get the police? I'd go but my head's bleeding and I have to take care of it."

Margaret looked confused. "Criminals here? And what happened to your head?"

"I saw two men climbing up the cliff. Their boat got damaged in the storm," he explained. "When I confronted them and tried to get them to stay here, they knocked me over the head. Harry saw what they did and he's keeping them in the storage shed. We think they're the ones involved in the insurance fraud."

"Is that what he got his rifle for?" Margaret rolled her eyes. "Fine, but it's getting dark and if I get attacked by some wild animal or some stranger…" She continued to grumble as she went to go put her boots on.

Edward didn't stick around to listen to her complaining. He went into the kitchen and pumped water onto the back of his head. Blood dripped into the sink. He touched the back of his head and felt a small cut there. It didn't feel that deep, but it was still concerning. He did his best to bandage his head and then walked back out to the storage shed, hoping the criminals hadn't made an escape while he was away. Harry was still near the doorway and Edward sighed with relief.

"You alright, Harry?" he asked.

"Just fine." He turned to Edward. "Your head?"

"Got a small wound there," he answered. "But I don't think I need to go to the doctor."

Harry nodded, then commented, "It's getting dark, Ed."

Edward looked out the door. The rain had stopped, but the sun was almost past the horizon and he was late in lighting the lantern for the night. He rushed into the lighthouse and started up the clockwork mechanism after lighting the lantern. When he came back down, he returned to the shed, where he and Harry continued to wait for Margaret to return with the police. After several more minutes, Edward looked out the door and saw Hanlon coming up the path with Margaret behind him.

"I got here as soon as I could!" Hanlon shouted, walking hurriedly up to him.

Edward stepped outside. "They're in here," he said.

"What happened to your head?" Hanlon looked at his wrapped skull.

"One of them hit me when they attempted to leave," Edward answered.

"The bastards," Hanlon grumbled as he walked toward the shed.

"Is it just you?" Edward asked, thinking it odd the man was by himself. "No other officers?"

"I ran out of the station as soon as Mrs. Bancroft told me what happened," he replied. "All of the other officers are out on duty anyway."

"He was the first one I spoke to when I got there," Margaret said.

"Luckily for you all I was working late," the detective said.

"Well, I'm going to bed," Margaret announced. "If you need me, don't bother bothering me." She turned abruptly and marched back into the house.

Hanlon stepped into the shed where Harry was still standing guard with his rifle. "Well, well, well," Hanlon smirked. "You gentlemen did a fine job rounding these two up."

"Detective Hanlon." Harry turned to him. "Good evening."

"A good evening indeed, Mr. Bancroft," Hanlon returned.

For some reason, Bert and Willie seemed to relax upon seeing Hanlon. Their faces even seemed to brighten and the small smile on Willie's lips didn't go unnoticed by Edward.

"And what happened to you?" Hanlon walked over to Bert and looked at his arm.

"That crazy old man shot me," he grumbled.

"He was about to attack us again," Harry stated calmly in his gravelly voice.

"You got the wrong men!" Willie exclaimed. "I want a lawyer."

"You can have a lawyer as soon as I take you down to the station. I'll even get you a doctor for your arm," Hanlon said as he nodded at Bert.

"We haven't done anything wrong," Bert defended them.

"You assaulted me." Edward glared at him.

"And you two are wanted men," Hanlon drawled. "Wanted for destruction of property, arson, compliance in insurance fraud, piracy, and murder. Should I go on?"

"What are you talking about?" Willie played dumb. "We didn't do any of those things."

"I took one glance at you and realized just how much you fit the description of our wanted criminals," Hanlon said. "The captain of the ship you set fire to gave us quite a lot of details of the three men he signed on to be part of his crew; three men who suspiciously disappeared after the fire started."

"We don't know anything about a fire on a ship," Bert said.

Hanlon ignored him and continued, "One was of average height, stocky build, brown hair, brown eyes." He looked at Bert then at Willie. "The other was tall, wiry build, dirty blond hair, blue eyes, and a scar on his left cheek."

"There are plenty of people who look like us," Willie protested.

"Maybe, but not all of them would knock someone over the head in an attempt to flee, now would they?" Hanlon asked.

"Sure we hit him, but he wasn't letting us leave!"

"I wasn't detaining you. You could have left without attacking me," Edward returned. Then he suddenly remembered something. "They had two bags with them too. They could have more evidence of their crimes in them."

Bert and Willie exchanged nervous glances. "Where are these bags?" Hanlon looked around at the storage room floor.

"They're probably still outside." Edward exited the shed and Hanlon followed.

The two bags were left on the lawn when the two criminals dragged Edward into the shed. Hanlon bent down and opened one of the wet linen bags. Inside he found some money, a tattered old photograph, and some other paraphernalia. Then something caught his eye. A silver trinket box lay at the bottom of the bag. It had an intricate carving on the front.

Hanlon turned it over and read the inscription on

the bottom. "Marlborough Smith Company. Mr. Ashman, do you remember the *Josephine*?"

"The ship that was ransacked and its crew murdered?" Edward recalled.

"Yes, that one." Hanlon stood up and handed Edward the box. "This trinket box was made by the Marlborough Smith Company. The *Josephine* was carrying several valuable items made by that same company when it was attacked. Coincidence? I don't think so."

"Dear God," Edward whispered as he studied the inscription on the back of the box. "It really is them."

Hanlon nodded and took the box back from Edward. He picked up the two bags and walked back to the shed. "You two want to explain this?" He held up the box in front of Bert and Willie.

"What about it?" Bert asked.

"Where did you get it from?"

"It was my mother's," Willie quickly stated.

"Was it now?" Hanlon shook his head. "This box was made by the Marlborough Smith Company. The very same company that supplied the goods aboard the *Josephine*, a ship you attacked."

"That… no… that was bought a long time ago," Willie stuttered.

"Alright, you two. You are officially under arrest for destruction of property, murder, piracy, and various related offenses." He walked behind them and took his gun out of its holster. "Start walking. I'm taking you down to the station."

"Shouldn't you get more officers first?" Edward asked.

"No, don't worry," Hanlon said with confidence. "I can take care of these two all on my own." He cocked his gun in show and pointed it at the two men. "Besides, I want these two detained as quickly as possible."

"I'll help you bring them to the station," Harry offered. "No use in you going alone; it's not safe."

"That's not necessary," Hanlon insisted. "These two won't be going anywhere if I'm around. Besides, don't you have a job to do?"

The tone irked Edward, but he explained, "It's okay as long as one of us is here to maintain the light."

"You two did more than enough with catching these two. No need for you to be further involved with these criminals," Hanlon said before commanding the two men, "Now start moving, you two!" He led Bert and Willie out of the storage shed.

"I'll just go with you." Harry turned to follow them out.

"No!" Hanlon yelled back. "I got it! Stay here!"

Edward and Harry were surprised by the man's aggressive tone. They exchanged glances, baffled by his irrationality.

"They could attack him if he's by himself," Edward said.

"He has more moxie than brains, I think," Harry agreed. "Did you tie the ropes well?"

"Made them tight and knotted several times," he answered.

"Let's hope that's enough," Harry stated. "And that Hanlon's a quick shot."

"I doubt he's as good as you," Edward snickered. "You could take the ass off a fly."

Harry laughed. "Let's go into the quarters. I want to take a look at your head, son."

Edward allowed Harry to lead him inside. He was still shaken by the event and rubbed at the back of his head, the pain still flickering through every now and then. He decided a bit of brandy would help take the edge off.

∾

Meanwhile, Hanlon was walking the men back to town through the path between the trees. He waited until he was out of sight of the lighthouse and keeper's quarters and near the edge of town before stopping.

"Can you untie me?" Bert groaned. "My arm is killing me."

Hanlon did as the man requested and did the same for Willie. He put his gun back in its holster. Willie stretched his arms while Bert went to check on his injury.

"So your name isn't really Cassinger, huh?" Willie sneered. "Detective Hanlon. So you were working with Howard the whole time and secretly against the police?"

"What the hell is wrong with you two idiots?" Hanlon growled. "I thought I made the plan abundantly clear. You two should have been halfway to New York by now!"

"The boat took on water because of the storm!" Bert yelled back.

"Then you should have waited until the storm cleared! Why the hell did you two think attacking the lightkeeper was a good idea?" Hanlon was seething. "Now they both know about you two and I look suspicious as hell coming here alone!"

"He saw us and was going to report our boat sinking," Willie tried to explain. "We could have gotten away, but we couldn't get out of the damn storage shed and then the other keeper showed up with a rifle."

"You should have just run for it when he saw you." Hanlon rolled his eyes. "Then on top of all of this, you actually have a piece of evidence on you that ties you directly to the crimes. Unbelievable." He shook his head in frustration.

Willie shrugged. "Well, I was going to sell that box for money once we got to New York."

Hanlon just glared at him and there was a moment of silence before Bert asked, "Say, how come you did come here alone? Wasn't there anyone else at the station?"

"There was, but I couldn't have them getting involved with this," Hanlon explained. "Now what the fuck am I going to do with you two?"

"We can still go to New York," Bert said. "Just don't tell anyone about us or what happened here."

"Well, that might have worked except the two keepers have to write a report about this now," Hanlon explained. "And don't you think it'll look a bit suspicious if there is a report about your capture, yet you two don't show up at the police station? How am I supposed to explain that?"

"I don't know why you had to go and get involved with this in the first place," Willie spat. "It was fine when it was just us and Howard."

"How do you think this whole operation got started in the first place?" Hanlon retorted. "Who do you think knows these upper-class ship owners? I know some rich bastard with a ship they want to damage, and I tell them I have men that can do it. All I ask for is a little bit off the top of their insurance payout."

"And why would they even agree to it?" Bert asked. "It's a big risk if they get caught."

"Extortion pure and simple." Hanlon shrugged. "For them there are bigger risks than insurance fraud, like ruined reputations. And do I hear stories. I got myself a young woman who just loves to share all the gossip. Got a child out of wedlock you don't want the neighbors to know about? I'll keep your secret. Have a mistress that you don't want the wife knowing about? I'll keep your secret. And in return for my silence, I get my share."

"So if you're the mastermind, why'd you get us involved?" Willie asked.

"Howard owed me a favor," he said. "I knew about his sordid past and had to erase some of it when he wanted a fresh start. I knew that he used to go around with you two and your *friend* that you murdered. Seeing how you both were still getting into trouble with the law, figured you wouldn't mind making a little money off it while you were at it."

Willie grunted. "Right, we made so much money after you were done getting *your* share."

"You should be lucky you two criminals even made as much as you did, especially with how badly you messed this up," Hanlon said. "And I still have to figure out what to do with you."

"Just say we escaped."

"I could, but once again, they'll wonder why I didn't bring more men with me," Hanlon countered. "You two have really fucked it up this time." He turned around and tried to think of a way out of this.

"Look, we're really sorry this got so out of hand," Bert said. "We'll figure this out."

"Nevermind, I already did." Hanlon pulled out his gun and turned around quickly, firing a shot into each of their skulls. "And I can't have you two fucking this up more than you already have. Sorry about that."

They dropped, dead in the dirt, blood pooling around them and shining like black water in the moonlight. Hanlon then lay down and hit himself hard with his revolver, making sure to leave a nice bruise before throwing his gun into the woods.

CHAPTER 14- AN UNUSUAL JUSTICE

Harry and Edward came down from the lighthouse the next morning to a very frantic Margaret. The woman was out of breath and rattling on about two dead men. It took both Harry and Edward to calm the woman down.

"What happened?" Edward asked once she had settled a bit.

"There's two men dead on the road!" she exclaimed. "I was going to get some goods from the store when I saw them. There were police all around them."

Harry and Edward exchanged glances, having a good idea who the two dead men were. "What did they look like?" Harry asked.

"I don't know, I couldn't get a good look at them," she said. "It looked like they'd been shot."

"What?" Harry was shocked. He looked to Edward.

"You thinking what I'm thinking?" Edward asked and Harry nodded. "I think I need to see this for myself."

"What's going on?" Margaret asked. "Does this have to do with the two men from last night?"

"There's a very strong possibility of that," Harry said.

☙

Edward had to walk nearly the full mile up the path that led to town to reach the scene of the crime. Several police officers were standing over the bodies making reports. "What happened?" Edward asked one of the men.

One of the officers looked up. "Sir, please don't come any closer."

Edward looked around him and saw that they were indeed the two men from last night. "Well, it's just those two men… they're the ones that attacked me last night. Detective Hanlon was supposed to bring them to the station."

"Do you work at the lighthouse?" the officer asked.

"Yes. After we caught them I sent my assistant's wife to get the police," Edward stated. "Where's Hanlon?"

"He's at Dr. Colson's," the officer explained. "When he was attempting to bring them into town, he said a third man, most likely their missing partner, came out of the woods. He grabbed Hanlon's gun and hit him with it. Then he must have shot the other two. You didn't hear the gunshots?"

"I vaguely remember a popping sound, but it was too far away to make it out clearly," Edward said, then asked incredulously, "But how could there have been a third man? There were only two. When I saw them on their boat there were only two. Then when they attacked me there were only two."

"He must have been hiding out in the woods then." The officer shrugged. "Did you hear them mention anything about a third man?"

Edward searched his memory. "No I didn't. But if that was their partner, why would he kill them?"

"Your guess is as good as mine," the policeman said.

Edward shook his head. "If Hanlon hadn't tried to take them in alone and taken our help when offered, this wouldn't have happened."

"You offered help?"

"Yes, Harry… the other keeper, he was willing to go with Hanlon to the station. He had a rifle, so he would have more protection," Edward answered.

"And he wouldn't take it?" The officer raised an eyebrow.

"No, he was pretty adamant about it," Edward said. "I mean I know their hands were tied, but still…"

"Wait." The officer put up a hand. "Their hands were tied?"

"Yes. When we had them cornered in the storage shed, I tied their hands with rope until Hanlon got there."

The officer looked dumbstruck. "Alright, I'll be taking a full statement from you and your assistant. I presume you'll be at the keeper's quarters?"

Edward affirmed that he would be, and later the officer came to take statements from him and Harry. They retold him the events of last night in as much detail as they could remember.

"One thing I can't wrap my head around is why their hands were untied," the officer stated. "I mean if their partner was going to just kill them anyway, why bother?"

Edward's brows stitched together. Hanlon had come alone, he had insisted they not help him take the criminals in, he seemed to be unsurprised by the ship explosion, even suggested there was a bomb... it suddenly all came together. "Because maybe it wasn't their partner that killed them," he said.

The officer looked concerned at the remark. "I would very much appreciate it if you both didn't discuss this case any further with anyone, please."

They agreed and the officer went on his way. Edward looked at Harry. "Hanlon was keeping them quiet."

"And if he was keeping them quiet, it must have been because he was working with them all along," Harry added.

"He had us all fooled."

"Well, let's hope the police put two and two together."

☙

Hanlon was sitting on his bed at Dr. Colson's house when Chief Bouchard came into the room.

"Chief?" Hanlon was surprised to see him.

"How you feeling there?" the captain asked, taking a seat in the room's visitor chair.

"Head's still sore, but nothing a day's rest won't cure." Hanlon gave him a weak smile.

"Oh, I am sure you will have plenty of time to rest." Hanlon didn't like the way his boss was looking at him. "But first, I just have some questions about what you told us this morning,"

"Alright," Hanlon sighed.

"So I had an officer speak to Mr. Ashman and Mr. Bancroft. They brought up some very interesting things." Something in his tone made Hanlon flinch.

"Like what?" Hanlon asked carefully.

"Like that both men had their hands tied together when you came to retrieve them," the captain remarked. "You didn't mention that."

"Well, I didn't think of it at the time," Hanlon said slowly. "But yes, they were."

The older man leaned back and considered for a moment. "So I wonder why then their hands weren't tied when we found them this morning."

Hanlon shrugged, feigning ignorance. "I don't know."

"I mean, if it was their partner that shot them, it doesn't make a whole lot of sense that he would untie them just to kill them."

Hanlon played the complying cop. "No, it doesn't." He took a moment to consider his next words carefully. "Unless that wasn't their partner at all. It could've been some crazy person hiding out in the woods for all we know."

"Could have been. Are you sure you can't remember anything defining about what he looked like?" Bouchard asked.

"It was getting dark. I really couldn't make out anything in particular; only that he was slightly taller than me. Otherwise, I couldn't even tell you if he had brown or black hair."

"Mm hmm." Bouchard nodded. "And there is one more thing."

"What's that?"

"You were offered help in taking the men into town by the two keepers, and yet you refused to take it," he remarked.

"Well, they aren't law enforcement," Hanlon defended himself. "I didn't think that they should have been further involved."

"That's fair, but you could have brought more officers with you in the first place."

Hanlon stopped. *I didn't think this through.* "Well, Mrs. Bancroft said they had *information* about the two men. I was not expecting them to be there," he lied.

"Did she now?" Bouchard said. "The way Ashman and Bancroft told it made it seem like she was perfectly aware they had actually captured the two men. Are you sure you heard her clearly? Or maybe you were so quick to get some fame and glory you wanted to take them in all by yourself?"

The wheels started to turn in Hanlon's head. Yes, it was better for his boss to think he was just after the fame than an accomplice to criminal activity. He hung his head in mock shame. "You're right," he said softly. "I just wanted so badly to bring those two in. I made a stupid mistake and now those two haven't been brought to justice."

Bouchard nodded. "And now we have a murderer on the loose." He paused before adding, "I think it's best if you take the next few days off to rest."

"I think I'll be fine," Hanlon protested.

"No, I have to investigate a few things," Bouchard countered. "Like how many officers were available last night that could have gone with you." He stood up and made for the door before turning and tipping his hat to Hanlon.

Hanlon just glared at him as he left. "God dammit!" he grunted. "Those sons-of-bitches ruined everything." Then he remembered the gun he had thrown into the woods. He needed to discard it if the police hadn't already found it. If they found it, they would know for sure he was lying. He'd wait till nightfall.

☙

"Margaret, stop it!"

Harry's yell got Edward's attention just as he was beginning to fall asleep. He walked over to the couple's bedroom only to see the older woman frantically running around, hurriedly packing her belongings into a cloth bag. Harry was arguing with her, trying to get her to stop.

"What's going on?" Edward asked.

"I'm leaving," she said breathlessly. "I can't stay here anymore."

"Why?" He was confused.

"Because she's losing her mind," Harry answered.

"More like I want to keep my sanity!" she yelled. "I think it's you two who have lost your minds for wanting to stay here. Have you forgotten everything that's happened? First, they find that dead man in the rocks, then that ship explodes, then Frances tries to kill the baby, and now those two men try to kill you before they're found dead themselves!" She pointed at Edward before declaring, "I don't want any part of it anymore!"

"Margaret, please." Edward tried to calm her down. "It's going to be alright. Yes, those things were horrible, but it's over now." Although he himself didn't quite believe that.

"No, it's not!" she cried hysterically. "This place is cursed! I just know it!"

"Margaret, would you listen to yourself?" Harry interjected. "There's no such thing as curses!"

"Yes, I'm listening to myself because I'm the only one making any damn sense around here!" she hollered. "And yes, there are curses and this place has one! But I'm not sticking around to find out who its next victim is!"

She finished her packing and roughly grabbed her bags off the bed and made her way for the door. Harry tried to grab her arm, but she pulled away. "Margaret, you need to stay."

"No, you can't make me!" she yelled. "Harry, you can come with me or stay here. But if you stay here and something bad happens to you, don't say I didn't warn ya!"

"But where are you going to go?" Edward inquired as he followed her out of the room.

"I'm staying with our son Donald. He already said he'd take me in," she responded.

"So you two made plans without informing me?" Harry looked angry.

"Because I knew you wouldn't understand."

"You're right," he commented. "Because I don't understand the ramblings of a madwoman."

"Go to hell!" With that she turned around and continued to yell as she made her way down the stairs. "Which is exactly where you'll go if you stay here any longer! Whenever you feel like using your heads, leave before it's too late!"

A loud bang resounded in the house when she slammed the front door shut. Edward turned to

Harry. "I don't understand. Last night she seemed like she couldn't care less and now she's terrified."

Harry didn't say anything at first. He seemed far older than he was in that instant. "If anything is going to be the death of me, it'll be her," he grumbled and shook his head as he retreated to his bedroom and closed the door.

Edward stared at the closed door and sighed. For someone who was of the no-nonsense type when it came to running a household, it was strange that Margaret would believe in something as fantastical as curses. But maybe she was right; he felt like he was losing his sanity because he too was starting to believe it. His head was swimming and he felt dizzy.

"Father?" He looked down and saw Marie and Anna standing together at the foot of the stairs.

"Sorry, girls," he said somberly. "It doesn't look like Margaret will be living here anymore."

The girls looked at each other and turned away with their heads down. Edward gripped the railing and hung his head. Margaret's words about the curse ran through his mind. A lot of strange things had happened: the dead man, the explosion, Frances trying to kill Thomas, the siren, Marie talking of spirit children, his encounter with Leonora, and now the two criminals and Hanlon. Hanlon. His stomach twisted in knots thinking about him. Edward wanted to do something about him, but he didn't have any concrete proof against the man besides a string of things that didn't add up. He could only hope that his comment about the third criminal not being the murderer put the right idea into the police's head about the detective.

Edward went to his room and slept. When he

awoke later that day, he didn't bother eating and went straight to start his shift. After a few hours, Harry came up earlier than when his shift was supposed to start. The older man said nothing at first and just sat in a chair. Edward knew he wanted to unburden himself, but he didn't press him. After several moments of silence, Harry finally spoke.

"Ed, as much as I gripe about that woman, I'd be dead if it wasn't for her." He sighed before continuing, "I can't believe she did this."

"Neither can I. But I guess she's just scared with all of the things that have been going on here." Edward leaned back. "Can't say I blame her, really."

"She was always strong-willed," Harry stated. "She would always put anyone in their place and now she runs."

"Because she thinks this is out of her control," Edward explained. "If she really thinks this place is cursed, then she can't do anything about that."

"I don't know if I should try to convince her to come back or just let her be," Harry wondered aloud.

"Maybe just let her settle down for now," Edward suggested. "You don't want to frustrate her anymore."

Harry nodded. "I don't think I appreciated her enough. I spent more time bickering with her than thanking her for all she did."

Edward realized that the statement was true of himself as well. "I know. She did so much to take care of the house and my children after Fran got sick. I never really let her know how grateful I was."

They were quiet for another moment before Harry spoke again. "What are we going to do now with both women gone? It's not like you and me can do it all when we have to work and the girls can only do so much."

Edward rubbed at his temple. "And my sister-in-law can't come all the time," he added. "She has her own house and family to take care of."

"And I don't know about you, but even pigs would turn their nose up at my cooking," Harry joked. "Oh hell, let's hire a maid."

❦

The night was pitch-black and a spray of stars crossed the sky. Wind whistled through the trees, an ominous sound. Hanlon stalked through the pines, stepping quietly around their twisted roots. He was using his lantern to try and spot his revolver, hoping the metal would shine. He felt like giving up, but after what seemed like an eternity, he saw something glinting out of the corner of his eye. Quickly making his way over to the spot, he breathed a sigh of relief when he found his gun. Soon he was making his way through the trees toward the shoreline. He'd dispose of the gun in the ocean and no one would ever find it, helping to validate his claims that it was stolen.

He stopped at the edge of the forest and looked up at the lighthouse. He watched it flash against the night sky and his fingers gripped tighter around his gun. *Ashman and Bancroft are up there now*, he thought. *If I'm going down, I should take them both down with me. They're the ones that couldn't keep their mouths shut.* God, he wanted to do it out of pure frustration, but he knew it would only lead to more questions for him. He was about to turn to throw his gun in the water when he was stopped by faint singing. He paused and looked around before seeing a fire on the beach. His heart began to beat faster in his chest.

"Who's there?" he called instinctively.

There was no answer, but the singing became louder and he felt himself being pulled closer to the beach against his will. He saw a woman standing on the sand and he found himself walking down the rocky slope to reach her.

"Who are you?" he asked, silently putting his gun in his pocket when he touched down on the beach.

"Does it matter?" he heard her silky voice reply as her singing ceased.

"Guess that all depends on why you're here," he answered.

"Why don't you tell me why you're here," the woman said as she walked closer to him. "I can't imagine you intend to use that weapon for anything good." She gently touched the area of his jacket where his gun was hidden.

"None of your business why I'm here," he said, withdrawing from her. He could now clearly see her glowing violet eyes and it startled him.

"Oh, are you sure about that?" She smiled at him. "I don't think Marie, Anna, and Thomas would be too happy if you took their father from them, especially after they lost their mother not too long ago."

Hanlon froze, his mouth agape. "How...how..." The words failed to come out.

She leaned in closer to him then whispered in his ear, "I saw what you did, and I know that you'd love to take them down with you."

He jumped back as she repeated the words he had thought of only moments before. She smiled terrifyingly at him. "Who are you? What do you want?" he asked, his voice quavering.

"I want you," she said, gently touching his face. "I need you."

"Get away from me," he said, pulling away from her hand.

"Why is it that you recoil from my touch, but not your mistress's?" she asked. "Only like married women?"

"How the hell do you know that?" he growled at her.

"Lustful men aren't that hard to figure out," she said. "Your sins are practically written on your face."

He stumbled back. "You don't know me; you have no idea about me."

"Oh, I have some," she said. "You have a lot of blood on your hands. I don't think you should add anymore tonight."

He just stared at her. "Why do you care?"

"I really don't," she lied. "But it will look oddly suspicious if both criminals and both lightkeepers are dead and you're the only one still alive. Why wouldn't the murderer come to kill you too?"

"You…you can't know all of this," he stuttered.

"Oh, I can." She walked up to him. "So why don't you forget about your plans for tonight and stay with me?"

"No, I can't," he said. He tried to walk backwards, but found he was unable to move.

"Yes, you can," she said seductively. "Just let yourself go." She gently pressed her lips to his.

He tried to pull away but he was overcome with desire as she started to hum. He pushed her down to the ground and knelt on top of her. A song broke from her lips and he was stopped in his tracks. His mind became clouded with unbelievable ecstasy. Elysia smiled, knowing she had him exactly where she wanted him.

CHAPTER 15- THE TRUTH UNFOLDS

The police were at the lighthouse for the second time that week. This time it was to recover Hanlon's body. Harry was the first to discover it when he came down from the light. He had noticed something on the shore in the watch room and walked to the beach only to discover the dead detective.

Upon looking at the body, Edward knew that no man had killed Hanlon. His cheeks were sunken in and his eyes were wide with terror. His skin was stretched taut and was dry like the sand he lay on. When one of the policemen lifted his shirt to check for wounds, his chest was sunken in with protruding ribs, as if all the breath in his body had been sucked out. The police were baffled as to how he could have come to be like this. They could not find the cause of death, only that he was dehydrated and emaciated—but how could that have happened overnight? What interested them even more was that the gun he supposedly lost to whoever had attacked him was sitting right in his pocket.

Edward was content to know that the police now knew Hanlon had lied. He also knew who Hanlon's murderer was and he went in search of her once the police had left. Elysia sat on one of the rocks, casually singing a lighthearted song and running her fingers through her hair. A small smile crossed her lips when she saw Edward approach from the corner of her eye.

"You killed him?" he asked point-blank.

"Maybe," she smirked. "Does that upset you?"

"I suppose any sort of murder upsets me," he replied. "But I guess he reaped what he sowed."

"Indeed." She turned to him. "Do you know what he came here for last night?"

"To get his gun." He shrugged.

"That, and maybe to keep you and Harry silent for good," she mused. "Looks like I saved *your* life too."

Edward raised an eyebrow at the thought of the detective coming to kill him. "Well, that's good to know. So you saved my son's life and now mine," he considered. "Why the sudden change of heart?"

"I'm allowed to change my mind, aren't I?" She smiled. "Besides, I have a feeling that detective made a nicer meal than you ever would have given his lust and greed. No offense."

"None taken," he mumbled under his breath. "So when can I expect to be made a meal of?"

"Oh, you need not worry anymore," she reassured him. "He'll fill me up for a while longer."

"Rather grotesque how it occurs," Edward observed.

"I suppose," she said. "But they don't feel any pain or horror until the final moment, if that's any consolation."

"Not really." He sighed once more. "Murder is murder regardless of how painless it may be. But it's not like I can bring you to the police, now can I?" He turned from her then and looked out toward the sea deep in thought.

"I wouldn't let you and you couldn't make me leave anyway." Elysia got up and walked toward him. "What else is troubling you?"

"A lot of things," he stated. "A lot has happened."

"And more will." Her voice turned grim. "It's not over."

"Why is it all happening now?" he asked. "Last year was quiet, nothing happened. Now everything is happening all at once."

"The tides are changing, the air is changing, I can feel it," she said, turning to the sea as well. "The spirits are growing restless. Something is going to happen soon, something drastic."

"What's going to happen?" His fear rose.

"I don't know. Perhaps the curse will finally be lifted," she replied.

"Curse?" He looked up at her curiously. "Before Margaret left, she carried on about this land being cursed."

"She's right." Elysia looked at him straight on. "This land has been cursed for many years. She was smart to leave."

"And how much do you know about this curse?" he asked.

"Not as much as I'd like," she replied. "You'd think with as long as I've been here I'd know a lot more by now."

"How long have you been here?" he inquired.

"I've never seen you until this year."

"What year is it again?" she asked.

"1898."

She thought before answering, "That means I've been here for about three thousand years now, I suppose."

He stopped, mouth agape. "You can't really be serious…"

"Oh, I am," she stated. "I've been here all along, but I don't always choose to show myself, usually only when I'm hungry."

"How did you come to be here?" he asked. "I can't imagine this is your original homeland."

"No, it is not," she explained. "I originally came from Anthemoessa, an island off the coast of what you now know as Italy. I lived with the other sirens, that is, until I was banished here."

"Why were you banished?" Edward was oddly curious to hear her story.

"I angered my father and was punished for it," she replied. "If you have read any of those stories that have been passed down through the generations, then you know the gods were vengeful, wrathful bastards." Her tone became angrier.

"What did you do?" he asked.

"My father was Achelous, the river god. He did something, something that hurt me, because he wanted to remind me of my place in the world," she answered. "So in revenge, I polluted his *precious* namesake river with the help of some of the humans who had their own contentions with the gods. Instead of killing me or transforming me into a tree or something, he decided to punish me by forcing me to stay here for all eternity."

"You can't leave at all?" he asked.

"No. I've tried and I can't. I can never get past the forest," she said sadly. "I've even tried just about every way possible to kill myself and even that never works. Death is the only salvation, and I will never receive it."

He couldn't help but feel pity for her. "I can't even imagine what it must be like to live in a place like this for three thousand years."

"The first thousand or so years were the worst," she continued solemnly. "Not a single soul here but me. Then once in awhile the occasional wayward Norse explorer or native hunter would show up and fall victim to me. More and more spirits came over the years. So now I'm the only one alive with a bunch of ghosts to keep me company."

She looked out toward the shore, a distant, sullen look in her eyes. Edward remembered Leonora saying she could only feel loneliness when it came to Elysia and now he could clearly see it. "I'm sorry, Elysia," he said genuinely. "Do all the people who die remain spirits here?"

"No," she said, turning back to him, the faintest hint of a blush on her face. It was the first time he had said her name and it meant he acknowledged her as more than just some vicious creature. "Some move on, others, usually those who die in a terrible manner, stay. Some are angry with me, of course." A small smirk came to her lips. "Seeing as I'm the one who put them here."

"Is Hanlon's spirit here?" He had to ask.

"Not sure yet." She smiled at him. "But I'll let you know if I see him."

Then he remembered the Varner children. "Do

you ever see two children, a boy and a girl?" he asked. "Brother and sister, they died here not too long ago."

"The two that drowned?" she asked and he nodded. "Yes, those two troublemakers like to play by the cave. That's how they died, you know? They were playing deep in the cave when a storm came. It flooded and the waves were too powerful for them; they couldn't get out in time. And the waves were even too powerful for me to do anything. When the storm subsided and the waters receded, I was the one who pulled both of them out so their parents could find them. Why do you ask about them?"

"My daughter, she…" He paused for a moment, a sudden chill creeping up his spine. "She said her sister was playing with them."

Elysia looked sternly into his eyes. "She shouldn't be." Her voice became serious. "Those two are dangerous. Most of the spirits here are."

"Why? What do they want?" he asked.

"They all want the same thing; they want what I want: to leave," she said. "They think lifting the curse will do that and maybe it will, but I'm not sure. They'll do whatever they can to lift the curse no matter what."

"What is this curse?" he asked. He was annoyed that he kept hearing about it, but never got any answers. "Does it keep the spirits here?"

"It appears that way. Spirits can become attached to any place, of course, but so many get stuck here because of the curse," she explained. "It also causes a lot of bad things to happen, which explains the events of late."

"How is it lifted?" he asked.

She didn't respond for a moment, then asked,

"Can I show you something?"

He considered for a moment, then nodded. She beckoned him to follow her and she walked behind the lighthouse to the far side of the rocks. She led him down a slope and over a few rocks, eventually reaching the opening to the cave. Edward slowed in his tracks.

"So this is the cave," he said. "I've never seen it before."

"It's usually well hidden with the rock I put in front of it." She sighed. "But the Varner children insist on making this their hideout." As she maneuvered inside she grumbled, "I hate coming in here." She felt uneasy whenever she was in the cave, always sensing something evil lurking in its dark depths. While she pushed herself to go in further, she realized Edward had stayed outside. She turned back to him. "Well, come on."

"I really don't know if I should follow you into that cave," he said, raising an eyebrow.

"Really now, Edward," she said with exasperation. "If I wanted to hurt you I would have by now." She walked deeper into the cave and he reluctantly followed.

Keeping his head down in the small space, he passed by the numerous items in the cave: the bottles, the coins, the mason jars. "Who put all of this here?" he asked.

"The Varner children did most of it," she answered. "But some of it was done by random others."

They walked deeper into the cave and Edward found it harder to see in the increasing darkness. He blinked several times, trying to get his eyes to adjust to the light. They rounded a corner and he jumped back in surprise. A middle-aged man was standing there, semi-transparent in appearance.

Edward was startled. "Who is that?"

"Another lost soul," Elysia said nonchalantly. "Shot himself here seventy years ago after he lost everything. I have to keep reminding him he's dead every time he starts raving about needing to go see his children."

The man suddenly disappeared from sight and Edward sighed with relief. Elysia finally stopped at a smooth, wide section of the cave wall. She held up her hand and it began to glow. The side of the cave was illuminated. Edward's eyes widened and he wondered just how much this woman was truly capable of. He looked at the cave wall and saw strange writing on it that was written in what looked like red paint.

"What language is that?" he asked.

"It's Phoenician," she told him. "A group of them sailed to these shores one day. One of them went into this cave and when he came out his eyes were rolled back into his head, his jaw was slack, and his hands were bloody. The others were horrified and had to snap him out of it. And on top of that incident, they found the body of another of their compatriots that I fed from only moments before. Needless to say, they sailed away in a hurry and I went in here and saw the writing the man left. I don't know what happened to him that possessed him to write it, but the message is quite clear."

"You can read it?" he asked, shocked.

"I can read many ancient languages," she said. "It speaks of the curse and how it leaves devastation in its wake and that in order for it to be lifted a sacrifice of light and life must be made."

"Sacrifice…" Edward's voice trailed off as he looked at the writing, realizing now that it was written in blood.

"Yes," she said. "Over the years several sacrifices have been made. Many of life, not many of light."

"What does it mean by light exactly?" he asked.

"Not sure," she replied. "I thought it could be something as simple as extinguishing a lantern or fire. I even thought maybe it was more metaphorical such as waiting for the sun to set, but no, none of that has worked."

"Then what?" he asked.

"I don't know, but I have a feeling we will find out very soon," was her eerie reply.

"Who cursed this land?" he asked curiously.

"I don't know if it was ever a *someone*," she said. "I always knew there was something wrong about this place from the very moment I was banished here."

"But how can that be?" he asked.

"I don't have all the answers," she said, and her tone turned more ominous, "but I know this place has been cursed for a long time. It even scares me sometimes."

"Scares you?" he asked, smirking at her.

"Yes, believe it or not, I can be frightened too," she said. "When I first came here, I might have been the only soul here, but I wasn't alone. There were shadows, dark entities if you will, all around. They lurked from the trees. They scared me. I had never seen anything like them before. They weren't human spirits or anything else I had ever come across. I don't know what they are or why they're here."

Edward felt his blood freeze. "They're...they're still here?" His voice quavered.

"Oh yes," she said. "They're always here. I call them the sentinels, because that's how they behave in a way. It's like they keep guard over this place, making sure that anyone who doesn't belong knows that they aren't welcome. Or at least that's the feeling they've always given me."

"I wonder if those were the shadows Leonora spoke of," he said absentmindedly.

"Who?"

"She's a fortune teller on the boardwalk," Edward explained. "She said that she saw two shadows leading my girls into this cave and then another taking my son out to the water."

"So she's a soothsayer?" Elysia was more familiar with the older term. "I had a feeling the sentinels were behind what your wife did."

"You're saying they made my wife try to kill our son?" His face grew long.

"Most likely," she stated. "She wouldn't be the first person they've influenced."

He just stared at the wall, obviously frightened. "Edward, you should leave this place," she said quietly. "It's not safe here."

"You know, you're the third woman to tell me that?" he said, offering her a small smile.

"Then maybe you should listen to us." She smiled. "Although I know you men don't very much like what we have to say."

He gave a small laugh. "I'll think about it, but I still have a job to do and a family to support."

She was silent for a moment, before speaking again. "Edward, I know how I've come across, and you probably think of me as nothing more than a vicious, ancient creature… but I…" She wanted to tell him that she was capable of love and that she felt it for him and didn't want to see him hurt, but she couldn't. She knew it would lead to nothing and so didn't see the reason for putting her heart in a vulnerable place. Instead she said, "But I am capable of feeling and I do have some morals. I know you're a good man and that you care about your family. So for their sake and yours, please, leave this place, before it's too late."

He looked into her eyes and felt the sincerity in them to his core. He nodded and she walked them out of the cave. As he made his way to the house, he greeted his two daughters, who were now outside playing. Their laughter echoed across the shore. Elysia viewed the scene from afar, a small tear falling down her cheek. The truth was, even if she hid herself from view, she was always observing what was going on at Wawenock Point, paying careful attention to those who came here. She had watched Edward and his family for the past few years and every day she came to love him more and more. He was handsome, but he was also strong and caring and protective of his family. She had resisted her feelings at first, but then she had decided to tempt him when she could wait no longer. She had lied when she said it was to feed off him; his death was not at all what she wanted. She had decided that if she couldn't have his heart, she would be content to at least have his body. But that too had failed when he proved to have even stronger moral fortitude than she had given him credit for. Of course she loved him all the more for his nobility. And now, when she had gotten so close to him, she would have to lose him. She didn't want him to get hurt and knew he would have to leave this place, but she would hate to see him go, the one tiny light in her dark life.

༂

Edward mulled over everything that Elysia told him. He thought back to when Frances had claimed to hear voices and it made him wonder if those voices were ever just in her head. He was determined to get answers as he traveled to Augusta. He entered the common room of the women's ward in the asylum and was surprised to see how crowded it was. There was a large number of female patients milling about and there didn't seem to be enough attendants to take care of them all. He spotted his wife and was pleased to see her sitting near the window instead of confined to her room. She was looking out at the yard below. He couldn't help thinking she looked like a bird in a cage and he felt a pang of guilt at the sight.

"Frances," he called as he approached her. She turned immediately and beamed at him.

"Edward! How good to see you."

He hesitated for a moment, not sure whether to hug her or not. He bent down to embrace her in order to let the awkwardness pass. She seemed put off by it at first, having gone so long without receiving such contact, but then returned the hug.

"How have you been feeling?" he asked as he sat in a chair across from her. "You look better." It was true. Her eyes were brighter and she looked well rested.

"Oh much better, really," she replied cheerily. "I

don't cry as often now and my appetite has returned."

"That's good, very good. You don't look so frail now," he commented, noticing the weight she had put on. She looked much healthier. "How have the doctors been treating you?"

"They're fine. They're very good at making me think clearly," she said. "But sometimes I think they lack, well, how should I say this, not so much compassion, but I suppose gentleness, a kind tone if you will. There's something distant about how they speak and act. There's a professional coldness to it."

"In other words, they have a terrible bedside manner," he offered.

"Yes, sadly," she agreed. "But I like some of the nurses I have. Some are very sweet, but others are very abrasive. Unfortunately, sometimes it's hard to get their attention. There are so many patients here that they can't keep up with us all."

"I've noticed." Edward looked around. "I heard they're supposed to be building a new hospital in Bangor. Hopefully that will help decrease the population."

"I hope so," she agreed.

"Do you have things to do here?" he asked, afraid she would be bored to tears.

"Yes. The nurses take me outside for fresh air and let me do some exercise here and there," she answered. "They've even encouraged me to do some knitting and other light work."

"That's good. It'll keep your mind preoccupied," he stated.

"There's even a band that plays on the lawn some nights." Then she added, "Oh, and the staff even took us on an excursion to the Isle of Springs."

"Oh really?" He was surprised they would take the patients beyond the hospital grounds. "That's some fine entertainment for sure."

"It was really beautiful. Now that I'm getting better I get to do more things," she explained.

"That's good. How has it been with your roommate?"

"We've been cordial," she explained. "But good lord can that woman snore. Some nights she's so loud I can't sleep."

"Have you asked to be moved to another room?"

"No. I don't think they can accommodate me," she said.

"I'll ask for you anyway," Edward said.

"Thank you." She smiled. "How have the children been?"

"They're fine. The girls miss you." He watched as her eyes got glassy.

She sniffled. "I miss them too. And I miss you."

He took her hand. "You'll be home before you know it," he reassured her.

"I feel so guilty not being there for them or to even help out around the house." She looked down.

"Well, Carrie has been coming to help every so often with the housework," he stated.

"Oh yes, she told me," she said. "She and Frank came to visit me."

"That was good of them." He breathed deeply as he absently ran his thumb against the back of her hand. "I need to ask you something, Frances."

"About what?" She looked at him nervously.

Without bringing up that fateful day when she tried to kill Thomas, he stated, "You remarked once that you had been hearing voices; that they told you to do things."

"Yes, I had." She frowned. "But I know they weren't real. I understand that now."

He looked at her carefully. Undoubtedly, her doctors had convinced her of such and perhaps it was for the best. But Edward knew better and wanted to tell his wife that she wasn't crazy after all; that the voices were real. But should he really say that and undermine all the progress her doctors had made with her?

"Humor me," he finally decided to say. "What did they say?"

She turned away. "It was too awful to repeat."

"Please, I need to know," he begged.

"Why?" she asked, confused why he would need this information now.

"I want to understand what … what it was like for you." It was a half-truth, he did want to understand, but he needed to know what these spirits were after.

"They kept telling me to sacrifice Thomas." Her voice became softer. "They kept telling me to take him to the waves and leave him there."

Hearing the word *sacrifice* made it all fall into place. Edward swallowed hard as he took in the fact that these spirits, or maybe it was the sentinels, wanted his son dead. "Did they ever say why?"

"Only that if I didn't, the world would be in danger," she said.

He pondered her answer. "Danger from what?"

"I don't know." She shook her head. "They never said. But they were so damned insistent. *Every single day* they would harass me."

"When did these voices start?"

"Not long after Thomas was born," she answered. "It started with barely audible whispers once or twice a day and I would just ignore them, thinking I was just hearing things, but then they started getting louder, more frequent, more demanding..." She started to sob. "I just couldn't take it anymore. That's why I did it. Oh, Edward!" she wailed. "I'm so, so sorry. I never wanted to hurt him, but there was no other way to make them stop. I love him, Edward, I really do." Now that she was thinking clearly, she could finally see that, yes, she had loved her son all along.

Her head fell into her hands and she cried profusely. *They were driving her mad*, Edward thought as he watched her. He rubbed soothing circles on her back.

"They caused all of this, didn't they?" he murmured.

She shook her head again as she sat up straight and removed her hands from her face. "No, I was already feeling melancholic even before the voices started," she explained. "But they made it worse, pushed me to do something I could never imagine." She inhaled deeply. "I don't hear them anymore. It was all in my head, you see. Some dark part of me that had been buried manifested itself during the course of my insanity. But I've pushed it away now."

He wanted so badly to tell her that those voices weren't imaginary and that they belonged to spirits who were preying on someone who was vulnerable, but decided against it. It bothered him that she thought those voices came from a darkness inside of her; that some hidden part of her had wanted to kill their son. He hated letting her feel guilty about what she had done, but she didn't need more confusion about her mental state when she was making such good progress.

"It... it wasn't your fault," he finally said. It was hard for him, part of him still wanting to blame her for not being strong enough to ignore the voices, but he also knew that she was ill and it was harder for her to fight them off.

"Yes, it was," she said sadly. "A real mother would have never done what I've done, no matter what was happening to them, but I let my illness get the best of me. My children deserve better than me."

"That's not true, and you'll have plenty of time to make it up to them when you come home."

"You're going to let me?" Her voice was so soft he almost didn't hear it.

"Frances," he lifted her chin, "I told you I wasn't abandoning you and I meant it. You made a grave mistake," he finally admitted. "But I know you're working hard on improving and when you're well enough you'll be able to come home."

"Do you think I'll come home soon?" She looked up at him with pleading eyes.

"I'll speak to Dr. Thornton and see how much longer he thinks you'll need to stay here," he responded.

She nodded. "I love you. And tell the children I love them, too, please," she begged.

"I love you too and I will." He leaned forward to give her a quick kiss on the forehead before saying goodbye. Then he went in search of Doctor Thornton.

The doctor was a young man, probably about Edward's age or younger. He walked with an air of confidence, but looked annoyed, no doubt from having to take care of so many patients. "Your wife is improving marvelously," he stated. "One of the best cases of recovery I've seen."

"Yes, I was surprised at the improvement," Edward remarked. "What's the worst of her symptoms at present?"

"Right now I believe it's the feelings of guilt she has," the doctor explained. "It is a predominant fixation in her thoughts."

Edward sighed. "Well, that's not surprising. She seems better physically at least."

"Oh yes. She has been eating regularly and sleeping well," Thornton remarked. "Though she does tend to take quite a few naps during the day."

"That's because the woman she shares a room with keeps her up at night with her snoring. Is it possible to have her switched to another room?" Edward asked. "I want her to be comfortable."

"I can certainly look into it," the other man answered. "See if anyone wants to switch rooms."

"Thank you. So when do you think she'll be stable enough to go home?" Edward inquired.

"If she continues as she has…maybe a few more weeks or a few more months," Thornton considered. "My concern is that if we allow her to go home too early, she will suffer a relapse. It's not enough to make sure that she is stable, but that she has a full recovery."

Edward nodded. "I understand, but I just feel so guilty about leaving her here."

"I would feel bad too if it were my wife," the doctor sympathized. "But think about how you'd feel if you took her home too early and she got worse again or did something awful."

Edward realized the doctor was right, but that didn't make him feel any better. The only consolation was that he knew she was safer here where the spirits couldn't harass her. As he left the hospital, he turned back and saw Frances at the window. She waved to him and he waved back, saddened that she couldn't come with him.

ॐ

"Can you feel it?" Sokondo asked Elysia while she was sitting on the rocks. The former hunter was the first of the Wawenock Indian ghosts to dwell here. He was speaking in his own language, which her gift for learning languages allowed her to pick up quickly in order to converse with him.

"Yes, it will happen soon," she replied as she turned to look at him. He appeared as he did when he died, the blood still coating the left side of his face where a gaping wound remained.

"I will be released soon, I know it," he said with conviction.

"Something is going to happen, but don't get your hopes up that it means you will be released." She stood up then.

"Hope is all I have," he stated in a forlorn voice.

He had become something of a friend to her over the years. Almost a millennia before the first European colonists arrived, Sokondo was killed here. He had been fighting with a man from a warring tribe and they somehow had made their way to the edge of the pine forest. The other man had bested him by hitting him in the temple with his club. While

Sokondo entered the spirit world that day and looked down at his lifeless body, Elysia seized upon an opportunity. Having gone several centuries at that point without feeding, she lured Sokondo's killer in with her song and consumed his energy, leaving behind a dry husk. Sokondo was grateful that his death had been avenged, but he had been afraid of Elysia for years, thinking of her as an evil spirit. Now he was one of the few ghosts here who didn't hate her as she had not personally dispatched him. Elysia always found it strange that no other natives had ever died here before him, but perhaps they knew something was wrong with this land and avoided it. It was therefore ironic to her that the area was named after them.

"The sentinels are restless," she declared. "Though I still don't know what their goal is."

"Maybe they are trapped as well," he offered.

"If that is true, then who trapped them?" she questioned, but secretly felt that the sentinels weren't waiting for their moment to be freed. Something deep inside of her told her they had their own agenda, but she couldn't figure out what.

"It matters not," he said. "As long as we are freed."

"I hope you get your wish," she said sadly. "I just wish I could get mine too."

"You will."

"I doubt it." She hung her head. "I am not of the spirit world like the rest of you. I was never even human."

"All the more reason for you to be released," Sokondo said. "You are not bound by the laws of the spirit realm."

"No, I am bound by the laws of the gods," Elysia reminded him. "I can't leave until they let me."

"Perhaps their influence has waned," he considered. "You have been here long enough. You have paid for your transgressions a thousandfold."

Elysia scoffed. "The gods can hold a grudge till the end of time no matter how much you atone."

"You must have faith," he said. "This is a different time now. The white men that came here no longer believe in your father. They have a god of a different name."

She considered for a moment. "I must admit that I feel his grip upon me lessening," Elysia said. "It used to be much stronger."

"See, now is the time," he announced.

Later that night, after Sokondo left her, Elysia ventured into the forest. She stopped at the rock she used to mark where her domain ended. She was never able to go past that point. Every time she tried she was pushed back, as if by an invisible force. Taking a deep breath, she took a step forward and then another step. One more and she would be past the boundary, free to roam wherever she wanted. Tentatively she moved forward and—she hit the invisible wall.

"Dammit!" she grunted. Why did she bother getting her hopes up? She should know by now that no matter how many years passed or how much her father's influence might have waned, she would never leave this place.

CHAPTER 16- CASE CLOSED

Edward went in search of Elysia the next morning after finishing his shift. He found her lounging on the beach reading a newspaper. "Am I really seeing a siren reading the *Kennebec Journal*?" he snickered.

She looked up at him and shrugged. "I like to keep up with current events. It's not like I get to see much of the world, after all."

"Is that last week's paper or this week's?" he asked as he realized he had left this week's paper on the kitchen table.

"Last week's. Don't worry, I took it from the waste pile," she answered as she read his mind. "I didn't go in the house."

He nodded and then remembered the portfolio of newspaper clippings that Marie had found in his office. He had seen it for himself and read through most of them. "So are you the one who's been keeping that pile of old newspaper clippings in my office?"

Elysia looked confused. "No, I don't know

anything about that."

"Maybe one of your ghost friends then?" he suggested.

"I guess," she said as she put the paper down. "So to what do I owe this visit?"

"I went to see Frances at the hospital," he replied. "She told me something interesting. She said the voices told her to kill Thomas because if she didn't the world would be in danger."

"Really?" That piqued her interest and she stood up. "So the sacrifice not only lifts the curse, but protects the world. But protects it from what?"

"Your guess is as good as mine," Edward said.

"If the sacrifice doesn't happen, the darkness will be unleashed," she said cryptically, a distant look in her eyes as if she suddenly had an epiphany.

"You know I hate when you talk like that," he muttered.

"The right moment is coming soon," she continued. "I think it's best if you aren't here for it."

"I'm working on that," he assured her. "In the meantime I'm going to head to bed."

"Sweet dreams," she cooed.

"Do me a favor and stay out of them please," he said.

She raised an eyebrow at him. "You've been dreaming of me?"

"Yes, and I don't like it," he murmured.

"Of all my powers, inserting myself into someone's dreams isn't one of them," she smirked. "I'm afraid that's all you."

His cheeks colored, and he looked down. That's what he was afraid she was going to say. "I should be going to get some rest," he said quietly.

"Try not to dream too much," she teased him.

☙

Carrie and Marie were chopping vegetables in the Ashmans' kitchen, preparing a stew for the family's dinner. The clicking sound against the wood was grating on Marie's nerves. She had barely slept last night. Thomas had had an upset stomach from the cow's milk and powdered formula combination he was given and kept crying. She had to stay up with him until he fell asleep again. She stopped cutting the potatoes and stared crossly at the knife in her aunt's hand.

"Marie, what's wrong?" Carrie asked when she noticed her niece's annoyance.

"I didn't get a lot of sleep last night," she murmured and returned to what she was doing.

"You need to sleep. You are a young girl," Carrie reminded her.

"How can I sleep when my brother won't shut up and I'm the only one here to take care of him?" she said tersely.

"Marie!" Carrie was surprised, having never seen Marie this angry. She was usually much calmer. "I know it's hard right now with your mother being gone, but he's only a baby."

Marie said nothing as tears formed in her eyes. She was tired … so tired. She was only ten years old, but with her mother and Margaret both gone, she had to play the role of caregiver to her brother and sister. Marie found it all so upsetting. She wanted to blame her mother for being sick, but she knew it wasn't her fault. She wanted to blame Margaret for leaving, but knew she was scared. She wanted to blame her father for not helping more, but knew he was busy with work. The situation couldn't be helped, but she just wanted to be a kid again.

Carrie saw her tears and stopped what she was doing. She bent down and put an arm around the young girl. "Oh dear, don't cry."

"It's not fair," Marie sobbed as she wiped her eyes. "I'm just a kid. I can't do it all."

Carrie knelt down and hugged her as Marie cried on her shoulder. "I know, I know. You don't deserve this, but it'll get better," she reassured her niece. "Your mother will come back once she's better."

"But what if she doesn't?" Marie sobbed. "What if she's stuck in that place forever?"

"She won't be. I've gone to see her myself and she's much better now than when you last saw her," Carrie assured her.

"Really?"

Carrie pulled away and gripped Marie's shoulders. "Yes, really. She will come home," she told her niece. "In the meantime, I'll talk to your father and see if there is anything we can do to try to make this easier, alright?"

Marie nodded and Carrie stood back up. "Now, my little trooper, wipe those tears and take some of that frustration out on those potatoes."

Marie smile and wiped her eyes with her pinafore before going back to helping with making dinner. She would have to bear this difficulty for now and just keep praying that her mother would come home soon.

꙳

Howard looked like a madman going through all of his records, finding ones that had any hint of proving relation to the insurance fraud. He stuffed them in his jacket pocket and then ran home to his house. He crumpled paper after paper, tossing the incriminating articles in the fireplace as fast as he could. The death of all of his cohorts had left him in a panic. He knew Hanlon was behind the murders of Willie and Bert, but he had no idea who had killed Hanlon. The papers described the discovery of his body like something out of a horror novel. He was terrified that someone had found out about their crime ring and decided to take their revenge. What if a family member or friend of a crew member of the *Josephine* or *Wade* had found out about them and was trying to get them back?

He was worried about the authorities too. They had found three of the perpetrators; it was only a matter of time before they connected the dots to the others. He was afraid either the police or someone else would get him. He decided to get out of town for awhile. He made up a story about needing to see his sick aunt in Boston. In a suitcase, he stuffed a few belongings and half of the cash he had made from the insurance scheme. The other half of the money he decided to hide under the floor boards just in case the police came to search his house.

At 4 p.m., Howard left his home and made his way to the nearest train station. He was paranoid the entire time. Every so often, he would look over his shoulder, feeling like he was being followed. Finally the train to Boston arrived and Howard quickly boarded it. He took a seat by the window and kept his head down. After several moments, Howard checked his watch. The train was supposed to leave ten minutes ago. What was the holdup?

Then a man boarded the train and sat next to Howard. Howard breathed in deeply through his nose, not wanting anyone to be near him. And of course the man had to start talking.

"Thought I wasn't going to make it," the man said.

"Good thing the train is running late," Howard commented, not turning to face him.

"Indeed," the man agreed. "Where you headed too?"

"Massachusetts." Howard didn't want to give too many details.

"Are you going to Boston too?"

Howard just nodded. He couldn't help but notice the man looking at him. The man kept talking. "I have to go that way to take care of some estate matters," he explained. "You see, my good friend is on his death bed and he is all alone in the world. I want to be there for him."

"I'm sorry to hear that," Howard said sincerely.

"Me too, he's a good man deep in his heart, but he lost a lot of people he cared about," the man stated.

"Did they get sick too?" Howard asked.

"Some, but most of them left him because he got into a bad crowd," the man continued. "He made a lot of mistakes; spent too much time with people who took advantage of him. Then he started doing the same thing to other people."

"Oh, that's a shame." Howard felt sorry for the man and couldn't help but think his story reminded him too much of himself. "I'm going to Boston to see my aunt. She's very ill as well."

"Oh, I hope she gets better." The man leaned back into his seat and then abruptly got up. "I forgot one of my bags. I need to get it before the train leaves." He then hurried out of the train car.

Howard looked at his pocket watch again. Why wasn't the train leaving? Howard looked up again and his heart sank as two police officers boarded the train with the same man he had been talking to. They walked right up to him.

"Howard Martin," the man announced as the two officers came forward. "We'll need to take you to the station to ask you some questions."

"For what?" He played dumb.

"Aiding and abetting in insurance fraud," the man answered.

"I have not the slightest idea of what you are talking about."

"Stand up, please," the man said, but Howard refused. The man signaled to the two officers and they grabbed Howard. "We'll also be asking you some questions about the murder of Detective Michael Hanlon."

"What? I had nothing to do with that!" Howard yelled as he was escorted off the train. "I haven't done anything!"

Down at the station, the police surprised Howard when they brought up his prior connections to Bert and Willie as a teenager. Most damaging were the records that they had found in Hanlon's house regarding one of the crimes that he had made "disappear" for Howard. Howard knew the detective was holding onto it for blackmail if he ever needed it. These developments, combined with much interrogation, broke Howard down. With the help of his lawyer, he was able to provide the prosecutors on the case with enough information about everyone involved, including the ship owners, to get himself a lighter sentence. He was also able to provide a sufficient alibi for where he was the night of Hanlon's murder, ruling him out as a suspect, much to the police's dismay. That crime would remain one of the most macabre unsolved mysteries in Port DePaix history.

CHAPTER 17- THE SACRIFICE

Two weeks had passed since Edward's conversation with Elysia. Surprisingly, nothing strange had happened at Wawenock Point since then. He hadn't seen much of the siren since he last spoke with her, but he occasionally heard her singing when he was up in the watch room. It was oddly comforting to him now, perhaps knowing that there was someone powerful out there able to protect them from whatever was lurking in the shadows.

He continued to visit Frances as well and with each visit she seemed to improve. The most telling sign of improvement was how she spoke. She sounded more and more like her old self and Edward was grateful. He was really hoping she could come home soon. The children missed her terribly, especially as the household was becoming harder to keep with both Frances and Margaret gone. Marie and Anna tried to pick up the slack, but they were just children and there was only so much they could do. Edward helped where he could, but it started to interfere with his work schedule. Hiring help was out of the question, the two keepers not being able to fund another person's salary. Carrie and Frank had been an enormous help, though, by bringing meals for the family once a week and sometimes taking their laundry to do with their own. It helped make it easier on the others.

Ultimately, Edward was hoping that the family would no longer have to stay here. He had requested to be assigned duties elsewhere. He had always thought himself a skeptical man, not easily swayed by superstitious nonsense, but he had seen too much and he now knew otherwise. He also thought it wise to listen to the many warnings he had received to leave. Perhaps it was Elysia's that had frightened him the most. The fact that someone as old and powerful as her could be afraid of whatever was out there frightened him as well.

Harry too no longer wanted to be there anymore with Margaret gone. He got grumpier and Edward could tell he was having a hard time fending for himself without his wife who usually took care of him. The couple wrote to each other, but Harry stayed quiet about what she said in her letters to him.

༄

It was the end of August and the family was preparing for a thunderstorm that night. It was expected to be a violent storm, not unlike a nor'easter. Marie tucked Thomas in as she had done every night since Margaret left. She gently kissed his forehead and laid him in his crib. She turned down the kerosene lamp before leaving the room.

Marie walked back to her bedroom and saw Anna staring out at the sky. Dark gray clouds were forming overhead as thunder rumbled in the distance. Out on the shore, the waves were picking up.

"Did you close all the windows?" Marie asked.

"Yes," Anna answered. "I saw them again."

"Saw who?" Marie could feel panic rising in her throat.

"Louise and Jimmy," Anna said. "They were looking up at the house from the shore before." The two spirit children hadn't been seen in weeks.

"Just ignore them," Marie said, trying to soothe her own fear. "They just want to scare you."

"Something bad is going to happen, I can feel it," Anna murmured, a blank stare on her face.

"Don't say that," Marie said sternly. "Everything will be okay."

Thunder broke out overhead and both girls jumped. A light drizzle began and the sky darkened some more.

~

The clap of thunder wasn't what woke her, but Frances jolted up in her bed at the asylum. She couldn't explain exactly what it was: a feeling, a vision perhaps? But she knew something bad was going to happen to her family. Rushing out of her room, she hurried to the nearest nurses' station. The nurses on duty that night looked at her pale face and wide eyes in concern.

"Mrs. Ashman, what's the matter?" one of them, Ms. Gibson, asked.

"It's... it's my husband and children, something,

something bad is going to happen," she explained in a hurried mess. "I just know it. Please, you have to do something."

Gibson was surprised to see Frances in such a state. Outside of crying, Frances was a model patient who never had these types of outbursts like some of the others. "Did you have a nightmare, dear?"

"No, well maybe, but it's just... please, I can feel it. Something isn't right," she pleaded. "I need to contact my husband."

"Mrs. Ashman, I don't think you'd want to cause him any worry," Gibson tried to rationalize with her. Patients with her type of insanity often suffered from delusions involving their family, though the nurse was confused about what could have brought it on now when Frances had been making so much progress.

"Please, can't you just send a telegram or telephone the police to have them send an officer to check on my family, please?" She was desperate at this point. "I know what you're thinking, but this isn't my insanity talking. In fact, this is the most strongly I have felt about something in months. Haven't you ever had a strong feeling about something and it turned out to be true?"

The nurse considered for a moment. She did indeed have those moments when her intuition was telling her something and it was right. And as she studied Frances's eyes, she saw how determined and clear they were. They didn't have that dull or saddened look that they normally had. If she hadn't known better, this was the look of a completely rational woman before her.

"Alright." Gibson nodded. "I'll see what I can do." She turned to the nurse at her right. "Ms.

Johnson, will you please escort Mrs. Ashman back to her room."

"Of course," the other nurse replied as she stood and led Frances back to her room. Frances knelt by her bed and prayed hard for her family's safety.

Meanwhile, Gibson attempted to make a telephone call, but no operators picked up, so she sent a telegram instead. But due to the storm, the connection was bad and it was never received.

༄

Meanwhile, Edward and Harry had just finished lighting the lamp for the night. Earlier that night, Edward decided to go outside to the storage shed to get more kerosene once he saw the clouds come in. If the storm was as bad as expected, the lamp would need plenty of kerosene to keep burning brightly all night. Edward sat with Harry in the watch room as night blackened the sky and rain continued to fall harder from the clouds. Another flash of lightning lit the sky, followed by a clap of thunder. Suddenly, a loud crack resounded in the tower and the floor shook. Both men jumped up, startled.

"What was that?" Edward asked.

"You don't think lightning hit the tower, do you?" Harry asked.

"Doubt it," Edward answered, looking out one of the windows. "It sounded like it came from below. Stay here, I'll check it out."

Edward hurriedly made his way down the spiral staircase, becoming slightly dizzy with the pace. He opened the door to the outside only to see rain coming down in torrents. He looked up at the light, but didn't see any signs of the tower being hit by lightning. He went around the base of the lighthouse and was shocked to see a large crack in the foundation.

"The hell?" he muttered to himself, tracing his fingers along the crack.

"It's happening," he heard a familiar voice call from behind him. He turned to see Elysia staring at him intently, fear ghosting her eyes.

"What's happening?" he asked, terror causing his heartbeat to increase.

"The curse," she said. "It will be lifted tonight."

"How do you know?" He froze.

"Look around you, Edward," she said, gesturing behind her. "The shadows have returned."

Edward forced himself to look and in that moment had never felt more terrified in his life. Sure enough, dark shadows were darting around between the trees. Some were running over the rocks. They seemed human in their movement, but Edward knew they were no such thing. They were something much more sinister.

"Elysia…" His voice caught in his throat and he felt the blood run from his face.

"Edward, you need to get you and your family out of here, NOW!" she commanded.

He ran back into the tower and ran halfway up the steps. He shouted to Harry, "Harry, you need to come down, the foundation is breaking!"

"What?" he heard Harry call back.

"Come down now!" Edward shouted as loud as he could.

He waited until Harry had joined him before both continued out of the light. "Mother of God," Harry whispered.

They both stopped dead in their tracks upon exiting. An angry-looking man stood at the entrance to the light and he was transparent. Looking out, they could see several more spirits standing around. All looking intently at the lighthouse entrance, but Harry and Edward had an odd feeling they weren't looking at them.

"Edward, you need to get your children and leave," Elysia stated as she came up beside him.

"What? Who are you?" Harry asked, startled at her presence.

"It's not important," she said. "But you both need to leave now!"

Edward agreed and made for the house.

☙

Marie was forced awake by a sudden tugging motion. She looked to see an old woman at the foot of her bed grabbing at her ankle. She screamed and jumped up. The old woman just continued to stare at her with dead, gray eyes. The woman had deep wrinkles and a sunken face.

"Anna!" Marie yelled.

There was no response from the other girl. Marie ran over to her bed with the intention of shaking her sister awake, but she found the bed empty. She looked back up to see the woman walking toward her. She decided to forgo finding her sister and ran out of the room and hurried down the stairs. Throwing open the front door, she saw the rain pouring down. She turned quickly to grab her shoes by the front door, only to see the old woman standing at the top of the stairs. Marie let out a shriek and darted out the door.

☙

Edward rushed toward the keeper's quarters to retrieve his children, but was met halfway by Marie. Tears streamed down her face and she was hysterical.

"What's happening?" she cried, running into her father's arms. "I'm so scared!"

"Where's your sister?" he asked.

"I don't know," she said. "I woke up and there was an old woman in my room trying to grab me. I just ran out here to get you!"

"I have to go get your sister and brother, go to Harry," Edward said, pulling Marie from his grip and jogging toward the house.

Suddenly, realization struck Marie once she saw the spirits. She ran and grabbed her father's arm. "No!" she cried. "The cave! They took her to the cave!"

"What?" Edward asked, not quite comprehending.

"The Varner children," Elysia filled in and he realized what was happening.

"But Thomas..." Edward trailed off, not sure which child to get first.

"I'll get him, you get Anna," Harry said as he met up with the others, and he ran into the house.

Edward ran for the far side of the rocks toward the cave with Marie hot on his heels, trying her best to pull her shoes on in the process. Edward pushed a rugged-looking ghost out of his way and it dissipated. Marie yelped and cried behind him, afraid of all the spirits. They passed several more, some more solid in appearance than others. They all appeared to be from different decades, however, and had either an angry or forlorn look on their faces. Many groaned and cried out for help.

When they finally approached the cave, the waves were rising and crashing violently against the rocks. The water came closer to the opening of the cave. Edward and Marie crawled down the rocks and stood at the opening of the cave. It was impossible to see in the complete darkness.

"Anna!" Edward called out.

"HELP!" was the bloodcurdling scream they got in response.

Edward squeezed into the opening despite whatever danger lay ahead. He turned the corner and found Anna being restrained by the two Varner children. Their spectral figures provided a dull illumination in the darkness. Anna was struggling unsuccessfully to get out of their grip.

"Let her go!" Edward yelled. He tried to push the children away from her, but they would not dissipate.

"We need her!" Louise yelled back. "I won't stay here another day!"

"You will not kill my daughter!" Edward yelled.

"We need to sacrifice her!" Jimmy yelled. "I don't want to be stuck here anymore!"

"Let me go!" Anna screamed.

The two would not let up their hold on her. Marie and Edward tried to fight them off, but were surprised at how strong they were. "No!" she screamed. "Papa, help!"

Marie and Edward grabbed hold of Anna, pulling her back as hard as they could. Out of nowhere they heard hissing and turned to see Daisy jump at Louise and claw at her. Louise screamed and released Anna. Edward and Marie took that as an opportunity to pull Anna out of the children's grasp.

They ran out of the cave just as a large wave crashed against the rocks. They were soaked, but clambered up the side of the hill as fast as they could. Daisy ran out of the cave and jumped up the rocks. Anna managed to grab the cat before she ran any further and held her close to her chest. She stroked the cat's fur as tears fell from her eyes. More waves came, nearly filling the cave with water. The angry shouts of the Varner children could be heard below as the family above ran back toward the keeper's quarters.

꒰ꇊ

Harry ran through the house up to Edward's bedroom. He heard Thomas crying from the outside. He threw open the door and was horrified to see a black shadow standing over the baby's crib. He could faintly hear words coming from the shadow, but he couldn't make them out.

"Get away from him!" he yelled and threw himself at the shadow.

The shadow rounded on him and pushed him to the ground. The shadow held him down and he found it hard to breathe. He struggled as hard as he could and looked around to use something to get the shadow off of him. He caught sight of the iron poker near the fireplace and edged toward it. As the shadow held tight to him he reached out as far as he could. Finally, he got a grip on the poker and flailed it at the shadow. The dark entity suddenly dissipated. Harry then remembered how Margaret once told him a story about how fairies didn't like iron; apparently neither did these shadow creatures. He kept the poker by his side and quickly picked Thomas up. He held the child tightly to his chest and tried to soothe him. He picked up a blanket from the bed and covered Thomas with it to keep him warm before heading back outside.

As he walked down the stairs he felt someone push him from behind. He dropped the poker as he stumbled forward and grabbed onto the railing, trying to regain his footing and not drop Thomas. He looked back to see a tall, burly man with black eyes standing behind him. The spirit's stare was of pure evil and terror shot through Harry. Thomas started wailing at all the sudden movements. Harry ran as fast as he could down the rest of the stairs, grabbing the poker in the process, and headed out the door. An angry shout came and he heard pounding footsteps behind him. He looked back to see the man standing in the doorway screaming at him.

~

Elysia stood near the door of the lighthouse and watched the scene before her. Several ghosts were staring at the lighthouse. The dark shadows were becoming more numerous. A low whisper rose from the crowd of spirits. Elysia felt her heart pounding, not sure what would happen next.

"You bitch!" she heard a man's voice call next to her. She turned to see a scraggly-looking sailor from the seventeenth century. "It is your fault I am dead!" he screamed and lunged at her but she quickly jumped out of the way.

"You caused my death as well!" another one of her victims screamed and pushed her from behind. She turned to see a pirate whom she had killed many years before.

"And me!" She turned forward to see a very angry Hanlon.

He jumped forward and grabbed at her throat. She tried to fight him off, but he was too strong. The other men were pulling at her, grabbing her hair and trying to hit her.

"Enough!" she muttered through gritted teeth. A brilliant white light emanated from her body and the spirits were thrown back. "You act like you didn't deserve what you got!" she screamed at them. She turned to the sailor first. "You killed your own captain when you got too drunk!" Next was the pirate. "And you, you killed so many to get yourself whatever riches you could find!" Then finally to Hanlon. "And don't even get me started with you!"

A sudden loud cracking sound stopped the commotion. Elysia turned to see another large fissure form in the foundation of the lighthouse. She also noticed the waves coming up higher on the shore. One came so high as to leave foam at the base of the lighthouse.

"*Mourez!*" Elysia heard a shrill scream in French from behind her. "*Libérez-nous!*" She turned to see a female ghost from the 1600s screaming at her. The woman had been a French colonist who drowned in a shipwreck.

The spirits crowded closer, making her step back toward the entrance of the lighthouse. They were all intently staring at her.

"Sacrifice! Sacrifice!" they began to chant in

various languages.

Elysia stared out into the crowd. Slowly, she realized just how exactly this situation would play out. She saw Edward, Marie, and Anna run back toward the light. Harry joined the group with Thomas in his arms. The rain was pounding down harder now and making it difficult to see, but Edward could clearly make out all the spirits.

"What's happening?" Edward called. He turned to see Hanlon, who glared at him. "Jesus Christ," Edward whispered.

"It's time," Elysia said quietly.

"For what?" Edward was cut off by another loud crack as mortar and bits of brick fell off the lighthouse.

Then came more chanting. "Sacrifice! Sacrifice!"

"Go on," Elysia said quietly to Edward. "Leave."

"What about you?" he asked, suddenly worried by her temperament.

"The sacrifice is going to happen," she said. "And I'm the only one here left alive."

"But you can't die." Edward was confused.

"Perhaps tonight…" She trailed off and turned toward the lighthouse.

The lighthouse cracked some more as a giant wave crashed against its side. The waves were becoming more violent. Water sprayed on those nearby. Elysia went to the door of the lighthouse and walked inside.

"Elysia, don't." Edward tried to get her to stop.

"Leave now," the siren said sternly. "I need to do this."

Edward watched as Elysia receded further into the tower. His attention was broken by a yell from behind him.

"Give us the child!" the sailor cried. The ghost jumped at Harry, trying to pry Thomas from his arms. The baby started to wail as Harry pulled back.

"Get the hell away!" Harry yelled as he thrust the poker at the sailor.

The ghost hissed as if burned when the poker touched his arm. Edward took his son from Harry and wrapped the crying child tightly in his arms.

"*Nous avons besoin de l'enfant!*" the Frenchwoman shouted as she too lunged for Thomas.

Edward turned his back on the ghost as Harry swatted her with the poker. "Why do they want him?" Edward yelled.

"I don't know, but they're not getting him!" Harry shouted back as he continued to push back the ghosts with the poker.

"We have to get out of here!" Edward announced over the wailing of Thomas and the chanting of the ghosts.

"Father!" Marie called to him. She pointed at the trees. "What are those?" Edward turned to see a line of dark shadows at the edge of the pine forest. It was as if the sentinels were standing at attention and waiting for something.

Harry pulled on his arm. "Ed, how are we going to get past them?"

"I don't know," he said in a faraway voice. "Maybe if we make a run for it?"

"Alright, not like I have a better idea," Harry said as he held the iron poker out in front of him. "On the count of three then, run as fast as you can." Edward held his son closer to his chest and Anna did the same with Daisy. Harry began the count, "One... two...

THREE!"

They ran as fast as they could toward the pine forest with the rain whipping their faces and mud splashing up at them. Ghosts reached for the family as they went, but they paid them no mind and rapidly moved past them. As they met the sentinels, Harry brandished the poker, fighting them off as they grabbed for the family. Harry, Edward, and Anna managed to break through the line, but Marie screamed as one of the shadows caught her. The family turned back to see a ghost hurl itself at the shadow, breaking its grip on the girl. Sokondo was holding back the sentinels, allowing the family to escape.

Using the little bit of English he knew, he shouted, "Go!" The family wasted no time following his command as they rushed through the forest.

Meanwhile, Elysia walked up the winding staircase of the lighthouse. Another crack resounded throughout the structure. The staircase rocked back and forth and Elysia stood still and grabbed tight to the railing until it stopped. She eventually made it to the watch room and looked out one of the windows. The storm was increasing in power. She urged herself to continue on, walking up the narrow staircase to where the lens was. The light was still burning brightly and emanating a strong beam through the dark and the rain.

Elysia walked through the small door to the outside deck. The rain pounded hard against her skin. She held tightly to the railing and stared out at the ocean. The angry waves were crashing higher now. One even reached the watch room deck below. The tower shook as another crack formed in the foundation. The spirits below were pushing against the lighthouse, helping it along. They continued to chant, "Sacrifice! Sacrifice!" Then Elysia felt the tower falling forward. An odd calm replaced her fear as she knew this was finally the end. All of her suffering would finally be over. She wouldn't have to stay in this cursed place anymore. She stretched her arms out to the sides and closed her eyes, taking a deep breath.

"Sweet death, take me," she whispered.

In that same moment the tower toppled over. But the calm she felt was fleeting and Elysia's eyes suddenly grew wide in fright. She let out a shrill scream as the lighthouse came crashing down.

On the ground, the family and Harry were fighting off spirits in the darkness of the forest as they made their way down the path that led to town. A few of the sentinels were hot on their heels. Anna turned back as one of the sentinels grabbed for her, but, as if by an invisible force, the sentinels were suddenly stopped from further reaching the group. The family stopped for a moment to observe the sentinels attempting to reach out for them but unable to get past the barrier. It was where their territory ended.

Just then, they heard Elysia's almost song-like scream. Edward's heart dropped knowing she was gone. The group could barely see it through the trees, but in that same moment, the lighthouse crumbled into the sea. The large waves swallowed the tower and it became completely submerged. The once proud light in the darkness was gone. An eerie blue glow emanated through the trees as the sea shined in a phantasmagoric light. One by one the spirits below were engulfed by a golden glow. Some, like the Varner children, breathed a sigh of relief as they were swept away to their respective afterlives. Others howled in agony as they were doomed to a more hellish fate. And Elysia's scream echoed through the night, a haunting melody.

CHAPTER 18- FROM THE ASHES

The district inspector and an engineer from the Lighthouse Service came the next morning. They stared mouth agape at the broken foundation of the tower. All that was left of the once prominent lighthouse was a base of crumbled bricks that looked like jagged teeth. The shoreline was littered with seaweed and driftwood as well, indicative of the large waves that had occurred last night. They couldn't comprehend how the tower had fallen into the sea.

"It was just inspected in July; declared to be structurally sound," the engineer said as he walked around the base of the tower.

"I know there was a storm last night, but no one else reported waves this high," the inspector commented. "I don't understand how the waves were this destructive here."

They continued to make notes for their report about the tower's condition when one of them saw a figure lying on the beach. "Hey, look over there! There's someone on the beach!"

The men rushed to where the figure was lying. A woman with long dark hair was face down on the beach. She was covered in cuts and bruises and her clothing, if it could be called that, was torn and tattered.

"Is she dead?" one of the men asked.

"Don't know," the other replied. He knelt down and lightly touched her arm. "She's warm," he declared then gently shook her arm. When she didn't move, he turned her over.

That motion startled Elysia awake. She instinctively moved away from them and stared at them with wild eyes, bewildered.

"Whoa, easy there, miss. We're not going to hurt you."

"What's going on?" she questioned. "Who are you?"

"We found you here on the beach, unconscious," the other explained. "We're from the Lighthouse Service. We came to investigate the damage done to the tower when we found you."

Damage to the tower? She looked to her left and saw the crumbled ruins of the lighthouse. It took her a moment to gather her thoughts. She had gone down with the tower the night before, hadn't she? She was supposed to be dead. Was this some sort of strange afterlife? Then she felt a stinging on her arms and looked to see that she had cuts all over the backs of them. She realized it must have been from the glass of the lantern room when the windows shattered after the lighthouse hit the water. Why would she have painful cuts if she was dead?

"I'm hurt..." she muttered. Whenever she had received a cut or scrape before, the wound would instantly heal—a curse of her immortality. So if her wounds weren't healing now…

"Yes, you got yourself quite cut up." Her thoughts were interrupted by one of the men. "I think we should take you to the local doctor. Here," he said as he took off his coat and placed it around her shoulders. "Do you have a name?"

"It's Elysia," she said slowly. "Thank you." She pulled the coat around her as she suddenly felt self-conscious, a feeling she had never quite experienced before.

"That's a nice name. You got a last name?"

"Uhm…" She hesitated. She had never had a last name; never needed one. So she played dumb. "I can't remember."

The men shared glances. "Do you remember how you got here?" the other asked.

She did, but there was no way she could tell them the truth. "I don't remember that either."

"Looks like you might have a case of amnesia," he explained. "If you bumped your head that could have caused it." She only nodded to that. "Can you stand?" he asked as he held out his hand.

"I'll try." She took his hand and stood on shaky legs. She pulled his coat tighter around herself as they led her up to the path to town. They wanted to take her to the local doctor, but what if she still couldn't leave? A hansom cab was waiting there and one of the men helped Elysia onto it. He sat next to her to accompany her into town while the other man stayed behind. He told the cab driver where to go and the driver jerked the reins to signal the horse to get going. Anticipation filled her as they made their way through the evergreen forest, going slowly on the muddy road.

She had only ever been able to go a few hundred yards into the forest before she would be stopped by some invisible force. But this time, there was no force stopping her as they made their way deeper and deeper into the trees. When the trees finally ended and the edge of town began, she knew she was finally free.

☙

The Ashmans and Harry had taken up in a local hotel the previous night. It was a small, cheaper one that sat further from the boardwalk. There was nothing special about it, but it was clean and the staff was accommodating when the family told them their harrowing story. Edward had sent out a telegram immediately after they arrived to the district inspector explaining what had happened. He must have sent at least five telegrams in total to clarify the situation, the man on the receiving end clearly not understanding or believing the gravity of the situation. He also wanted to make sure that they understood the conditions of the storm last night made it impossible for them to stay at the station. Otherwise, he and Harry could be reprimanded for leaving their post. Eventually, the inspector said he and an engineer would come out in the morning as soon as possible.

The two men attentively listened to what Edward and Harry had to say, making notes for their official records. After taking an account of everything that had happened, they went to investigate the scene themselves. When the men left, Edward decided to rest in his hotel room. He had only gotten an hour or two of sleep last night with how wound up he had been. It was around two in the afternoon when the inspector came back with the engineer. Edward and Harry listened with rapt attention as the men explained that the lighthouse was completely destroyed. Then the inspector asked Edward something curious.

"Did you have any visitors or other family members staying at the quarters?"

"No, it was just my children, Mr. Bancroft, and myself. Why?"

"Well a young woman was found lying on the beach today. She was badly cut up so we took her to Dr. Colson on Parker Street," he replied. "She said her name was Elysia, but couldn't remember anything else. Poor woman must have hit her head and gotten amnesia. Do you know of any such person?"

Edward paled. So she had survived after all. His heart leaped at the thought, and he had the urge to go see her. But how could he explain to them that this woman was a siren who had sacrificed herself for them? He looked at Harry, hoping he would know what to say. The older man just shook his head and Edward followed suit.

"No, I cannot recall ever meeting anyone by that name," Edward replied.

"Me neither," Harry chimed in. "Wonder how she got there?"

"Hopefully her memory will come back to her. Until then, do you two have anywhere to stay until we can figure out this whole situation and bring you other work accommodations?" he asked.

"I have family members nearby," Edward answered.

"And I have children I can stay with," Harry said.

"Very well, I will be in touch. Good day, gentlemen." He tipped his hat to the two keepers and left with the engineer.

"So she survived," Edward said quietly.

"Who was she anyway, Ed?" Harry asked. "You two seemed to know each other."

"Normally, I wouldn't think you would believe me, but after last night, I don't see why you wouldn't." He sighed. "She's a creature that used to instill fear into the hearts of sailors. One that is as ancient as Greece itself…. She's a siren, Harry."

Harry looked at him incredulously. "You can't be serious?"

"I'm afraid I am," he stated. "She's been haunting those shores for over three thousand years, or so she claims. She's the one who stopped Hanlon when he came back to cover his crimes."

"You mean she's the one who…?" He trailed off. "How do you know all of this?"

Edward chuckled. "She tried to tempt me on several occasions, until she realized she couldn't win me over. She's the one who told me about the curse."

"Curse? Peggy talked of a curse before she left."

Edward nodded. "Guess she figured it out too. I suppose that's why the lighthouse fell into the sea and it's why the siren sacrificed herself; to lift the curse." Edward shook his head. "I need to see her, Harry. I have so many questions."

"I do too, but after what she did to Hanlon, I don't think I'll be going near her again."

༄

Edward made his way to the home of Dr. Colson,

the town doctor. He knocked and Mrs. Colson answered the door. She perked up when she recognized Edward.

"Ah, Mr. Ashman," she greeted. "Come in, come in. We heard what happened to the lighthouse. You weren't injured too, were you?"

"No, no, I'm fine, just a little shaken," he replied. "But I was told a young woman by the name of Elysia was taken here?" He stepped into the parlor, which had a gaslight chandelier and an ornate oriental rug.

"Oh yes, she is upstairs resting. Do you know her?" the woman answered. "Poor thing can't seem to remember anything. My husband said it's probably from the bump to the head she received."

At first he wanted to say he did, but realized that if the district inspector came to check on Elysia, the Colsons might tell him that Edward was here and that he already knew the injured woman. So he continued to play dumb. "No, but I was curious as to who she was and what happened to her. And being in my position I can't help but feel that I failed to help someone in distress."

"I understand, but let me ask my husband if she can accept visitors." The woman disappeared for a moment before returning. "Yes, you can see her, but make it brief, she needs her rest."

Mrs. Colson led Edward upstairs. She explained that they reserved a room in the house for the worst injured patients who were unable to reach the hospital. She knocked on a door to their left when they reached the second floor.

"Elysia, dear, may I come in?" she called into the room.

"Yes," was the soft reply.

Mrs. Colson opened the door to reveal Elysia standing by the window looking outside. "You have a visitor," the older woman announced. "This is Mr. Edward Ashman, he's the keeper at the lighthouse you were found at."

Elysia straightened and turned. Her eyes grew wide when she saw him. "Edward?" she asked in disbelief.

"Yes," he said, trying his best to hide his smile. She had a cut on her lip and forehead and likely had more scrapes and bruises hidden beneath her clothing and bandages. She was wearing a loose-fitting quarter-sleeve dress, likely one of Mrs. Colson's own, and had bandages wrapped around her arms. But at least she was alive.

"He just wanted to ask you some questions if that's alright?" Mrs. Colson asked.

Elysia nodded. They heard Dr. Colson call from downstairs and Mrs. Colson left to attend to him.

"You survived," Edward said with a small smile as he walked over to her.

"I did." She looked down. "I'm not sure how though or why. Going down with the tower like that should have killed me."

"What do you remember?" he asked.

She breathed deeply and went to sit on the bed. "I went outside on the deck of the top floor. I felt relief at first as the tower gave way, but then as I was falling into the water, this sudden vision of sorts struck me," she said in a faraway voice. "I can't remember what it was about now, but it terrified me and I screamed."

"I heard you," Edward said as he sat next to her.

"Then there was a sort of strange calm that came over me when I was in the water and this bright light engulfed me," she explained. "Then that was it; I must have passed out. I woke up on the beach this morning. I don't know how I got out of the water or how I ended up on the beach … or how I'm even alive."

"And you were taken here? So you're no longer cursed to stay at the Point, then?" he asked as the realization came to him.

"So it seems," she said.

"Sounds like a miracle."

"If that's what you want to call it," she grumbled.

He knitted his eyebrows. "You don't think so?"

She shook her head sadly. "I was ready to die, Edward. I wanted it to finally be over with. I was ready for my suffering to end, but now … I don't even know what to do. I … I'm not even *me* anymore."

"What do you mean?"

"Look." She held up her bandaged arms. "I'm all cut up. In the past, I was never able to get hurt like this. Anytime I would get a cut or a scrape, it would heal instantly. I even tried to do other things I used to, like how I can create light with my hands, but nothing … I think I'm just human now." She started to cry. "I didn't want this, Edward. I didn't want my miserable existence to continue, but here I am."

He tentatively put a hand on her shoulder. "Elysia, I can't begin to imagine what your life must have been like for all those centuries, but think of it this way, you have a second chance now. You're no longer forced to remain in exile. You're free. You can do all sorts of things you couldn't before and you don't even need any powers for them."

"But for what?" She sounded angry. "What am I

supposed to do now?"

"Living a regular human life will take some getting used to, but I'll be here to help you."

"You will?" She looked up at him in surprise. "But why would you even want to help me?"

"You saved my life and my family's life. I think I owe you something for that."

Elysia felt more tears come to her eyes as she saw the sincerity on his face. This was why she loved him; he was kind to a fault. But he belonged to another, and she could never have him. Perhaps that was another reason death had looked so appealing. She would still be alone even among a thousand people.

"Thank you," she said quietly.

There was quiet between them for a moment, before he asked, "So do you think it worked? Do you think the spirits left?"

She shrugged. "I'm not sure. I mean if I'm not cursed anymore, then it should logically follow that they aren't either."

"I keep wondering how the curse came to be in the first place," Edward pondered. "Do you think your father had a hand in it?"

"I wouldn't be surprised, but I suppose we'll never know the true origins of it," she said. "But I think it was tied to me all along. I was the first soul there. It makes sense then that the first soul would also be the last to give up their life, in a manner of speaking. I know I didn't die, but when I gave up my old self and was finally freed, I guess that freed everyone else too."

"Hard to understand it all," he murmured.

Elysia sighed, "So what do I do now?"

"Well first, you need to heal. You were pretty

badly injured," he said. "Oh, and we'll need to come up with a back story for you."

"Back story?" She looked confused.

"Something to tell people when they ask who you are," he replied. "You'll need a last name, a *believable* age, where you're from, all of that."

She groaned. "My head hurts enough already, do we need to add to it?"

He chuckled. "It's only going to help you, especially if they start asking how you ended up stranded at Wawenock Point."

"I suppose exiled by a god thousands of years ago isn't very realistic to most people."

"Afraid not." He paused then added, "And I already said I didn't know who you were, so that's really going to make people wonder why you were there in the first place."

"Can't we just say I got stranded there during the storm when I was out sailing?"

"That might work, but then they might start asking questions about what happened to your boat and why a young woman was out sailing by herself."

She rolled her eyes. "I think it's best if I just keep saying I can't remember anything."

He smiled. "I guess that'll do for now until we can think of something better."

Just then Mrs. Colson returned. "Sorry to cut this meeting short, but I think you should be getting some more rest dear."

"Right, you need to worry about getting better," Edward played along. "I'm sure your memory will come back in time."

"Is there someplace I can find you at, Mr. Ashman?" Elysia asked. "In case I remember something."

"Well, I still have to figure out where I'll be staying myself," he replied. "But I'll let Mrs. Colson know where you can find me."

"Thank you." She smiled at him.

"I'm just glad to see you're alright." They stared at each other for a moment, perhaps a bit too long, before he made his exit.

EPILOGUE

One Year Later

Autumn graced the Maine landscape as the builders worked on the new lighthouse being built near the spot where the previous one had stood. Everyone was confounded by how the old tower had suddenly collapsed into the sea. Inspectors, engineers, and architects alike found it hard to believe that the storm caused its destruction when the structure had been previously deemed sound. Then again, no one believed the former lightkeepers either when they told them how high the waves had risen.

They decided to build the new light a few feet back from where the old one previously stood, just in case another storm hit. The new light was almost completed, just a bit more to do. The current builders still found bits and pieces of the old structure. They would wash up on shore every now and then. They would also find old coins, buttons, and bottles and could never figure out where they were coming from.

George Dorsett, one of the builders, decided to go exploring on his lunch break. He walked near the far side of the rocks, feeling himself being drawn to the area. He climbed down the rocks and was astounded to see an opening in the side of the cliffs. Being a tall man, he had to stoop down to enter into the cave. A humming noise caught his attention and he went deeper and deeper into the darkness.

As their lunch break ended, the rest of the workers went back to working on the new tower. Two of them climbed the scaffolding to work on the upper parts of the structure. The foreman called out for George, who was supposed to be helping with this part.

"Hey, George!" he yelled. When there was no response, he turned to the builder next to him. "Where'd he go?"

"Don't know," the other man replied.

"I saw him go that way," a third builder called out and he pointed to the far side of the rocks. "He didn't come back?"

"Doesn't look like it."

The foreman decided to go find his missing worker and went to the far side of the cliffs. He looked down only to see the missing worker sitting on one of the rocks.

"George?" he called to him. There was no response. "George!" Still nothing. He turned to one of the other workers who had followed him. "What's he gone deaf?"

The other shrugged, but yelled out loudly, "GEORGE!"

When the man on the rocks still did not

acknowledge their presence, they climbed down the cliff. George wasn't known to ignore his boss or fellow workers. He tended to keep to himself, but was good-natured and hardworking. His current behavior gave them cause for concern. As they reached him, the worker asked, "Hey, George, didn't you hear us call—"

The men stopped dead in their tracks when they finally faced him. George sat on the rocks with his eyes rolled back into his head, jaw slack, and bloody palms resting on his knees face up.

"Holy hell," the worker murmured.

The foreman shook the unresponsive man's shoulders. "George!" he yelled. "George! What happened to you?"

When he still was unresponsive, the foreman slapped him hard across the cheek. That seemed to do the trick. He blinked and his eyes faced forward again, but he seemed dazed and disoriented. Then he started to babble something.

"What are you trying to say?"

"They want them," was his slurred answer.

"Who wants who?"

"Must bring them back."

Unable to get a sensible answer out of the man, two of the builders took George to Dr. Colson while the rest resumed their work. They didn't know what happened to George in that cave and when he finally came back to his senses, he said he couldn't remember even going in there, only that he had seen the opening in the cliffside. A few of the men were brave enough to go into the cave, thinking perhaps someone was hiding in there and had hurt their coworker. But they saw no one there and left without gaining any further insight into what had happened to George. None of them, of course, had bothered to look at the smooth section of cave wall to see the message George had left in his own blood under the Phoenician writing: "They belong to us."

☙

Marie and Anna ran across the grass of their new home and jumped into a pile of leaves, their giggles dancing on the night air. Thomas wobbled behind them. The boy was becoming an expert at running. Edward sat on the porch, watching his children. He was soon joined by a much happier and mentally sound Frances. She touched his hand and he placed his other over hers.

"Thomas is growing very strong," she said, smiling at her husband. "Just like his father."

"And as resilient as his mother," he replied. He smiled back at her and silently rejoiced at having his wife back. She was very much like the wife he remembered when they were first married and he couldn't be more grateful.

Frances was finally able to bond with Thomas, but she felt guilty for missing out on the early months of his life. She was more hopeful and happy now and felt like herself again. Sometimes she would have negative feelings and thoughts, but she did her best to push them away. Needless to say, she decided she would not be having anymore children, as she did not want to risk suffering from the same illness again.

Edward had gotten a new job as a clerk for a local dry goods merchant. He refused to ever work as a lightkeeper again, preferring to stay on the mainland.

The family lived in a nice house on the edge of town now after having stayed with Edward's brother for a few months after they had vacated the keeper's quarters. It wasn't anything fancy, but it had a spacious yard and more than enough rooms for all of them. The girls were happy about each getting to have their own bedroom for a change.

Then there was Elysia. Edward kept in contact with her to make sure she was getting along alright. She was settling into her normal human life as well as one could hope given her circumstances. They decided to tell everyone she was the daughter of Italian immigrants who died on that fateful night last year. The story they came up with was that she and her parents were out sailing when the storm rose up. They were unable to make it back to port and their boat capsized. She was separated from her parents, who were presumed drowned; neither they nor their boat were ever found. Elysia somehow managed to survive, ending up at Wawenock Point. When Edward went to find out who she was, he felt so bad for the stranded, parentless woman, he had to help her. He set her up with a woman who ran a boarding house and that's where she currently stayed. He even taught her some basic skills so that she could get a job. And God help him, but he still had dreams of her. Given her loss of powers, he realized that she hadn't been lying when she said they were the products of his own imagination. He felt guilty about it, of course, but after all, it wasn't like he could control what he dreams about.

During the summer, he actually had the chance to introduce the former siren to his family. He and Harry ended up receiving silver life-saving medals after review of their efforts with the ship explosion was made by the Secretary of the Treasury. Edward hadn't seen much of Harry since that night when the tower fell. The man decided to retire altogether and live out the rest of his days with one of his children, claiming that he had "seen enough horseshit for one lifetime." He had reunited with Margaret as well.

The awarding of the medals took place at the Port DePaix town hall. Edward and Harry were dressed in regular suits, having traded in their navy blue uniforms. Their wives and the children, dressed in their best, had come out for the event. Unfortunately, half the damn town had come out to see it as well. The hall was packed with everyone wanting to see the local heroes and the papers had sent out reporters to cover the ceremony.

"Christ, the press is here too," Edward muttered to Harry. He felt sick with all the pomp and attention he was getting.

"Must be a slow news day," Harry commented as he rolled his eyes.

The mayor and one of Maine's representatives from Congress were there. The representative came to the podium and spoke. "Today we are here to recognize the efforts and bravery of two men of this community, Mr. Edward Ashman and Mr. Harry Bancroft. On behalf of the Secretary of the Treasury, the medal we will be presenting them both with is the silver life-saving medal.

"On the night of July first, 1898, both Mr. Ashman and Mr. Bancroft were serving as keepers at the Wawenock Point Light Station. On that night, a passing cargo ship suffered an explosion that caused extensive damage to the ship and injured several of the crew members, seven of whom lost their lives that day. Without hesitation, and with disregard for their own safety, Mr. Ashman and Mr. Bancroft proceeded into the water to rescue the shipwrecked crew. Together, they pulled seven men out of the water. One man may have drowned and one more may have succumbed to his injuries had Mr. Ashman and Mr. Bancroft not acted as swiftly as they had. They both upheld the longstanding tradition of humanitarian service and putting others before themselves."

Applause broke out in the room and the representative pinned the medals to Harry's and Edward's jacket lapels. Edward made eye contact with Frances, but she just smiled. The representative shook hands with both men, as did the mayor. Edward went back to his family after the ceremony was over and saw a familiar face coming toward him.

"Congratulations, Mr. Ashman," Elysia greeted him.

"Miss Marino," he returned. "It's good to see you here."

"Of course, I had to come," she said. "Is this your family?"

"Yes, this is my wife, Frances, my daughters, Anna and Marie, and my son, Thomas." He introduced them all, acting as if she didn't already know.

"A pleasure to make your acquaintance." She smiled at them. Marie, however, looked at her curiously, feeling she had seen the woman before.

Frances asked, "Oh, my husband told me about you. He helped you after you lost your parents, correct?"

"Yes, I didn't know anyone in town and was of

poor means without my parents, but he helped me though I was but a stranger," Elysia replied.

"I'm sorry for your loss and I hope you are faring better now," Frances offered.

"Thank you and I am," Elysia said. "Well, I just wanted to come to congratulate you." She turned to Edward briefly before turning back to Frances. "You're very lucky to have such a good man."

Frances seemed a bit taken aback by the comment. "Oh, I know," she stated quickly.

"And I'm glad to have finally met the beautiful family he talks incessantly about," Elysia said to reassure her. "And I can see why. Good day to all of you."

As Elysia walked away, Frances muttered to Edward, "You didn't mention how pretty or young she was."

"I didn't think it mattered," Edward said. "I was just helping someone in need, nothing more."

She quirked an eyebrow at him, to which he gave her a "really" look. Elysia made herself rare though, sometimes meeting Edward in the park after work if she needed help with something or just wanted to say hello. It was hard for her to adjust to her new human life, considering she now had to follow proper rules of etiquette and even her bodily functions had changed. She might have been able to bear it all had it not been for *him*. It was agonizing for her; being so near to Edward, but never close enough.

But still, she was trying to make the best of the situation and partake of the opportunities her new life afforded her. She was baffled by the world she currently lived in. Being isolated for so many centuries, she was, for the most part, only ever able to read or hear about new technologies and events. Now she was able to experience it all for herself and she was astounded by how far humanity had come and yet how, at their core, humans hadn't really changed.

☙

Sunset had come over the coast and the last of the builders were leaving for the night. They didn't like staying at Wawenock Point past sundown. They always felt that they were never alone when building the new lighthouse. And after what happened with George today, they especially did not want to be there when it got dark. After they had gone, strange, almost animal-like sounds could be heard coming from the darkness of the cave. The spirits had all moved onto whatever beyond they were destined for last summer when the lighthouse had fallen, but the sentinels had stayed and continued their watch over the shore… and waited.

HISTORICAL NOTES

This story came about from my love of lighthouses and all things related to the seashore. I chose the 1890s as this is a time before lighthouses became automated and lighthouse keepers were still a necessity. At its peak, the state of Maine had about eighty lighthouses. Although the lighthouse in my story is fictional, it is inspired by the many Maine lighthouses that sit atop rocky cliffs at the edge of pine forests. Likewise, Wawenock Point and its respective town of Port DePaix are fictional. The 1890s also have a nostalgia that I thought was fitting for the story. It allowed me to include old-time entertainment like fancy ice cream parlors, boardwalk amusements and rides, and vaudeville shows.

Lighthouses existed in the United States before it became a nation, with Sandy Hook Lighthouse in New Jersey, built in 1764, still the oldest operating lighthouse in the country. Earlier lighthouses were originally illuminated with either wood, coal, or candles until gradually a combination of oil lamps, metal reflectors, and poor quality lenses were used. The invention of the Fresnel lens in the 1820s improved illumination immensely. In the United States, keepers had a variety of duties. Their main concern was keeping the light on from sunset until dawn. They also had to keep records of daily shifts, absences, the condition of the light station, the weather and water conditions, use of supplies and expenses, shipwrecks, and any unusual occurrences. They had to clean and make repairs to the lighthouse equipment and other parts of the light station when needed. They were also expected to intervene with shipwrecks and to help people in distress when able. Family members could help maintain the light if the keeper was unable to fulfill his or her duties. By the 1880s, electricity started to be used to power aids to navigation. Eventually, all lighthouses were automated, ending the need for lightkeepers in the United States.

Another aspect I added to this story, and greatly expanded upon from the first draft, was postpartum depression (PPD) in the nineteenth century. During this time, the illness was known as puerperal insanity. The medical community usually divided it into three stages: insanity of pregnancy, puerperal insanity, and insanity of lactation. The most common was puerperal or parturition insanity, which was believed to start one to six weeks after birth. The insanity could take on either a manic or melancholic form. This is where our current understanding of PPD differs from the nineteenth century understanding. While many physicians noted the depressive symptoms associated with PPD, they also noted that the manic form of the illness was more prevalent. In this form, the patient would exhibit symptoms such as incessant talking, restlessness, refusal to eat, obscenity in language and behavior, and even hallucinations and delusions. Some of these symptoms would be more in line with what we call postpartum psychosis today. Puerperal insanity would generally be treated at home in mild cases or in asylums in more advanced cases. The treatment would include adjusted diets, warm baths, purgatives, use of tranquilizers and sedatives, light work and exercise, isolation from family and friends, and, thankfully, kindness and reassurance.

While delving into this mental illness, I brought the nineteenth century asylum into the story. In the early nineteenth century, reformers like Dorothea Dix attempted to instill "moral treatment" into the American hospital system. The insane had previously been kept in harsh conditions with the use of restraints and isolation. "Moral treatment" attempted to bring kindness into the treatment of the insane with the use of recreation, work, and privileges. Furthermore, Dr. Thomas Kirkbride believed the appropriate settings with natural light and fresh air could help cure the insane as well. Public asylums with large wings and windows to let in sunlight and air sprang up in nice, secluded areas. At these "Kirkbride style" institutions, patients could hope to be cured through socializing and occupational therapy.

Very soon, the state-run hospitals encountered the problems of underfunding, understaffing, and overcrowding. As a result, many asylums fell into a pattern of patient abuse and neglect. Yet other institutions seemed to escape this cycle. This appears to be the case of the Maine Insane Hospital which, at least at the time my story takes place, seemed to be of the better sort. The hospital opened in 1840 and by the turn of the century, it was reported to be clean and gave much attention to the recreation of its patients. The biggest complaints regarding the asylum, at least from what I could find, were the outdated wards and overcrowding. The asylum, like many others of its kind, now stands mostly abandoned in Augusta.

ACKNOWLEDGMENTS

I wrote the first draft of this story when I was still in college; my form of escapism, I suppose. I once again would like to thank my parents, Darlene and Bill, who made sure I didn't lose my passion for writing and helped me fine-tune this story. I would also like to thank my other family members and friends for supporting my writing career, especially Cynthia Youngclaus, who again was my beta reader. To my former French teacher, Leslie Holleuffer, thank you for reviewing my French translations. I would also like to thank William Thiesen and the United States Coast Guard for answering my questions about the operations of the United States Revenue Cutter Service. Also, thanks to Jeff and the United States Lighthouse Society for all of the resources they provide. Finally, thanks to Christine LePorte for editing my manuscript.

ABOUT THE AUTHOR

Genavieve Blackwood is an author of historical and horror fiction. She has Bachelor of Arts degrees in political science and fashion studies from Montclair State University, where she honed her writing skills. She continues to use her writing to help people suffering from mental health issues. She previously published *Wanderer Among Shadows*, based on the true story of one family's struggles during the Salem Witch Trials. For more information go to www.genavieveblackwood.com.

Printed in Great Britain
by Amazon